Roberdeau Buchanan

Life of the Hon. Thomas McKean

Roberdeau Buchanan

Life of the Hon. Thomas McKean

ISBN/EAN: 9783337055363

Printed in Europe, USA, Canada, Australia, Japan

Cover: Foto ©Raphael Reischuk / pixelio.de

More available books at **www.hansebooks.com**

LIFE

HON. THOMAS MCKEAN, LL.D.,

MEMBER OF THE CONTINENTAL CONGRESS FROM DELAWARE,
CHIEF JUSTICE AND GOVERNOR OF PENNSYLVANIA,
SIGNER OF THE DECLARATION OF INDE-
PENDENCE, AND PRESIDENT OF
CONGRESS.

COMPILED FOR THE GENEALOGY OF THE McKEAN FAMILY.

BY ROBERDEAU BUCHANAN.

WITH AN INTRODUCTORY LETTER

BY THE

HON. THOMAS F. BAYARD, LL.D.,

LANCASTER, PA.:
INQUIRER PRINTING COMPANY.
1890.

LIBRARY
UNIVERSITY OF CALIFORNIA
DAVIS

O

INTRODUCTORY CORRESPONDENCE.

THE AUTHOR TO THE HON. THOMAS F. BAYARD, LL. D.

WASHINGTON, D. C., *December* 23, 1889.

To the Hon. Thomas F. Bayard, LL. D.

Dear Sir:

Having in course of publication a *Life of the Hon. Thomas McKean, LL. D.*, who for a number of years was the "leading delegate from Delaware" in the Continental Congress, and also a Signer of the Declaration of Independence; it would give me much pleasure if you will permit me to dedicate the same to you, as a slight mark of my appreciation of the services you have in later days rendered, in many important positions, not only to the State of Delaware, but to our country at large.

I have the honor to enclose proof pages of the work as far as yet printed; and, with your approbation, will from time to time send the succeeding pages as they are received from the printer.

I have the honor to be, with much respect,

Yours very truly,

ROBERDEAU BUCHANAN.

REPLY OF THE HON. THOMAS F. BAYARD.

WILMINGTON, DEL., *March* 25th, 1890.

Dear Sir:

Since receiving your letter of December 23d, the proof sheets of the "*Life of Thomas McKean, LL.D.*," have been duly sent me, and I now congratulate you upon the successful completion of your labors.

I accept with pleasure the honor of your dedication, and as an American, especially as a citizen of Delaware, I am justly proud to be thus associated with the Memorial of a patriot, statesman, and jurist, so distinguished as Thomas McKean.

In this State Mr. McKean commenced his professional and public career; as a Representative of this community he was delegated, together with his compatriot, Cæsar Rodney, to the Stamp Act Congress of 1765; and from that time onward until American liberty and independence were firmly secured, he was

(v)

continuously invested with the highest public trusts which the people of this State could bestow; all of which he executed with a fidelity and ability which awakened the grateful admiration of his constituents, and secured for him the highest popular esteem.

To him is due the high distinction of serving longer and more continuously than any other member of the Continental Congress, in the stormy and eventful years of the struggle for our independent National existence.

To this it may be added that his assiduity was equalled by his courage, discretion and ability in the "times that tried men's souls."

In parliamentary bodies, declamatory vigor and selfish assertion, contenting itself with sharp criticism upon the work of others, may, and often do, give distinction and sometimes an undeserved reputation with the public; while the patient, self-controlled and steady labor that formulates and constructs is recognized and appreciated only by the "singular few," who quietly take part in the real work of State building, and to whom mankind are chiefly indebted.

In this sober class of unselfish and conscientious constructors of our republican system, Thomas McKean must be ranked among the first.

As his kinsman and descendant, you have performed a pious duty in compiling with simple accuracy, a full and faithful record of the life-work of your ancestor; and the picture you have given of his private as well as of his public character and career is just and true.

As a citizen, you have done public service in contributing an important chapter in the veritable history of laying the foundations of the government whose blessings we now enjoy, and which it is the duty of each of us to assist in transmitting unimpaired to posterity.   I am, dear sir,

Respectfully and truly yours,

T. F. BAYARD.

To Roberdeau Buchanan, Esq.,
Washington, D. C.

PREFACE.

As a contribution to the Revolutionary history of our country, with which his life was so intimately connected in many exalted positions during half a century, this biography of the Hon. Thomas McKean is given to the public. As originally written, it was accompanied by a genealogy of his descendants; but on account of the prominent part that Governor McKean bore as one of the framers of this government, his biography therefore becomes of interest beyond the limited sphere of a genealogy, and is now published separately.

In the biography of Governor McKean, the author began by taking Sanderson's fine biography as a foundation, but soon rejected that plan, and quoted the work with other authors ; he has reluctantly been obliged to transpose Sanderson's biography and rearrange it so as to place the facts in chronological order, as well as to bring together all the writers upon one topic before taking up the next. This comparison of various authors has been the means of correcting several mistakes in Sanderson which have been copied by all succeeding biographers (Appendix II). By the use of some extraneous matter, and explanations, have been brought into a connected account, several topics that in Sanderson's biography seem to have no connection. Minute details, so far as accessible, poetry, anecdotes, and other trivial matters often neglected by the severe historian, have been made use of; for it is these unimportant matters which make us feel acquainted with another, and give a clearer insight into his life and character.

Of the signing of the Declaration of Independence,—an intricate subject, which has been discussed by many able men, including Peter Force, Webster, Winthrop, Bancroft, and lastly Judge Chamberlain, it is belived that an abstract of all that has been written upon the subject is here given.

Through the courtesy of the Assistant Secretary of State, and the other gentlemen, the author has been accorded the especial privilege of photographing the original Manuscript Journals of Congress in the handwriting of Charles Thomson—an especial favor, since these Journals are among the most valuable records in the archives of the State Department, and have never before been reproduced in fac-simile. Doubtless but few historians have seen the originals, since permission from the Secretary of State is required even to inspect them; and trusting to the inaccurate published copies, many writers have been led into error, or else have found discrepancies they could not explain. It is hoped, therefore, that these fac-similes may help to elucidate matters, that long ago should have been made clear.

Permission to photograph the Journals was given while pages 39 and 45 of the present work were being set in type; and merely a few verbal changes could be made in the text. It was found subsequently that the negatives were too delicate to be photo-lithographed; they were consequently reproduced by the Moss process in New York.

The first fac-simile is the Rough Journal, with the Declaration of Independence displayed, reduced three-eighths size. Here may be seen the wafers attaching it to the page—the names of John Hancock and Charles Thomson *in print*—and at the top of page 95 of the Journal, the following clauses *omitted in the printed copies*:—

"Ordered That the declaration be authenticated & printed
"   That the committee appointed to prepare the declaration superintend & correct the press."

It will be noticed, that the names of the fifty-six Signers, and the clause preceding them in the printed journals, are nowhere to be found. Compare the fac-simile with the text opposite.

The second plate is a portion of the above on a larger size, and from a second negative, half size.

The third plate is the page of the Secret Journal relating to the engrossed declaration, half-size; the interlineation is plainly seen. By comparison with the printed journal, the latter will be found faulty in the kind of type used, as well as in spelling.

Several offices and appointments held by Governor McKean, and other facts not heretofore mentioned in his biographies, are

here given ; and at the cost of some repetition, the numerous
estimates of Governor McKean's character, by various authors,
have all been inserted; but scattered through the biography to
avoid weariness to the reader. An apology may be due for the
long accounts of the impeachment trials, of Mr. McKean's seat in
Congress, and perhaps some other portions that may appear tedious.
They are retained here, hoping to make this biography of Governor McKean a standard, wherein may be found, in full, all information that is known of him and that has appeared in print.

To the Hon. William F. Wharton, Assistant Secretary of State,
and to Frederick Bancroft, Esq., Chief of the Bureau of Rolls and
Library, the author is especially indebted for their concurrent
permission, to photograph the manuscript Journals of Congress,
for copies of letters, and for much other information officially fur-
nished from the Department records. And in no less degree is
the author indebted to S. M. Hamilton, Esq., of the Bureau of
Rolls and Library, for facilities in making the above mentioned
photographic negatives; and also for opening to the author's inspection not only the original Articles of Confederation, but also
numerous letters and papers of the revolutionary period, in the archives of the Department, and for much information, unofficially
and very cordially given.

WASHINGTON, D. C., *November,* 1889.

CONTENTS.

THOMAS McKEAN.

THE subject of this biography[1] was the son of William McKean and Letitia Finney, of Scotch-Irish ancestry. He was born in New London township, Chester county, Pennsylvania, March 19, 1734, old style. After an elementary instruction in reading, writing and arithmetic, Thomas and his elder brother Robert were, at the ages of nine and eleven years respectively, placed under the tuition of the Rev. Francis Allison, D. D., a man of character and reputation.

STUDIES LAW.

After passing through the regular course of instruction here, and acquiring a knowledge of the practical branches of mathematics, rhetoric, logic, and moral philosophy, Thomas went to Newcastle in Delaware, and entered the office of his relative David Finney, as a law student. Some months after, he engaged as clerk to the prothonotary of the Court of Common Pleas; a situation which enabled him to learn the practice while he was studying the theory of the law.

So great was the reputation that Mr. McKean acquired in his youth by his industry and talents, that before he had attained the age of twenty-one years, he was admitted[2] as an

[1] The basis of this biography is *Sanderson's Biography of the Signers*, 2d edition, Philadelphia; published by Brown and Peters, 1828. Robert Waln, Jr., is the author of many of the biographies in Sanderson, including that of Thomas McKean. The author is much indebted to Sanderson's Lives, yet the extracts from that work form but a small portion of the present biography, in which are quotations from about two hundred other works. Several mistakes in Sanderson are here corrected. Robert Waln, Jr., above mentioned, was the son of Robert Waln, of a Quaker family, member of Congress 1798–1801, and was born in 1797. He was an author and poet, and died at an early age in 1824.

[2] 1754, J. Hill Martin, *Bench and Bar of Philadelphia*, 1883, and *Penn. Mag.*, v., 489.

attorney at law in the Courts of Common Pleas for the counties
of Newcastle, Kent, and Sussex, and also in the Supreme
Court. Before the expiration of a year he obtained a considerable share of business, and in May, 1755,[1] was admitted to
practice in the courts of his native county of Chester. He was
also admitted to the courts of the city and county of Philadelphia. In 1756, the Attorney-general, who resided in
Philadelphia, appointed him, not only without any solicitation,
but without any previous knowledge on his part, his deputy, to
prosecute the pleas of the crown in the county of Sussex. He
resigned this office after performing its duties for two years
with judgment and ability. In 1758,[2] April 17, he was admitted to the bar of the Supreme Court of the province of
Pennsylvania. The envy which the success of the young
lawyer occasioned among his professional brethren, merely
served as an additional spur to his industry, and increased his
assiduity in the pursuit of legal knowledge ; for though he had
become the eloquent advocate and able lawyer, he was still the
close and industrious student.[3] He afterwards went to England and studied at the Middle Temple, being admitted there
May 9, 1758.[4]

As a recreation from his studies, in 1757, December 28, Mr.
McKean enrolled himself with about one hundred and twenty-
five others "in Richard Williams' company of foot, whereof
William Armstrong is colonel, in Newcastle county."[5] In the
same year he was elected clerk of the House of Assembly, an
honor of which he was unapprised until he received information of his appointment from Benjamin Chew, at that time
speaker. The following year he was again elected ; but after
serving that term he declined further appointment. In 1762,
he was selected by the legislature, together with Cæsar Rodney,
to revise and print the laws passed subsequent to 1752; a duty
which they speedily and satisfactorily executed.

---

[1] *Penn. Mag.*, v., 139, 244, 489, xi., 249 ; and *Hist. Chester, Del. Co.*, J. Hill
Martin. Not 1756, as given in *Sanderson.*

[2] *Penn. Mag.*, v., 489, and *Bench and Bar ;* not 1757, as in Sanderson.

[3] Judson's *Lives.*

[4] *Penn. Mag.*, v., 244–5, 489 ; xi., 249 ; *Bench and Bar*, p. 22.

[5] The original paper in possession of J. Henry Rogers, Esq. See also
Life of George Read, W. T. Read, p. 48.

THE ASSEMBLY OF DELAWARE.

In the same year Mr. McKean first embarked in the stormy sea of politics, which he continued to brave for nearly half a century. In October, 1762, he was elected a member of the Assembly from the county of Newcastle, and was annually returned for seventeen successive years. So much attached to him were the people of that county, that they continued to elect him, although for the last six years of this time he was residing in Philadelphia. He still however retained his house in Newcastle, probably because his business frequently called him to that city. Finally, on the 1st of October, 1779, on the day of the general election in Delaware, he attended at Newcastle, and in an address to his constituents, declined the honor of further re-election. He was then waited upon by six gentlemen in the name of the electors, who asked him to name seven persons suitable for representatives. He replied that he knew not only *seven*, but *seventy*, whom he considered worthy of their votes ; but the request being repeated, he acceded and wrote down seven names. The election resulted in the choice of the seven gentlemen whom he had named.

HIS MARRIAGE.

On Thursday the twenty-first of July, 1763,[1] Mr. McKean was married to Miss Mary Borden, eldest child of Col. Joseph Borden, of Bordentown, New Jersey. She and her sister Ann, who married Francis Hopkinson, were said to be two of the most beautiful ladies in New Jersey.[2] Of her family and ancestry I have found as follows :

THE BORDEN FAMILY.[3]

RICHARD BORDEN, born 1601, married Joan (born 1604; died July 5, 1688), settled with his wife in Portsmouth, R. I. He purchased land in New Jersey in 1667, and died May 25, 1671, leaving with other children:

BENJAMIN, born in May, 1649, at Portsmouth, R. I. He

---

[1] Not July, 1762, as stated in *Sanderson's Lives.*

[2] E. M. Woodward, in Bordentown *Register.*

[3] Compiled from Savage's *Genealogical Dict. of First Settlers; Gen. Dict. of R. I.,* John O. Austin, 1887; *Hist. Burlington and Mercer Cos.,* E. M. Woodward and John F. Hageman; *Hist. Bordentown and Burlington,* in Bordentown *Register,* 1876, E. M. Woodward; Keith's Provincial Councillors, 1883, p. 269.

was married at Hartford, Ct., September 22, 1671,[1] to Abigail Glover, born 1653[2] (daughter of Henry Glover, of Hartford, Ct., born about 1614; died 1689, and of Abigail his wife), and removed to Shrewsbury, N. J. In 1716, he deeded lands to his son Joseph, of Freehold. His Bible record is contained in a Concordance of the Holy Scriptures, etc., 1698, now in possession of Oliver Hopkinson, Esq., of Philadelphia. On the fly-leaf is written "Benjamin Borden, His book, 1706." and below, "Abigal Borden died 8 of Geneyery in 66 year of her age and year of our Lord 1720." The date of his marriage, and birth and death of his son Joseph, are verified as here given in the text. Benjamin Borden died in 1718 or later, leaving eleven children, of whom the seventh child was:

JOSEPH, born May 12, 1687, probably near Freehold, and when about thirty years of age removed to Tamsworth's Landing. He was married about the year 1717 to Ann Conover (formerly *Covenhoven*), of Monmouth county, New Jersey. By deed, March 3, 1724, he purchased of Samuel Tamsworth one hundred amd five acres of land, and subsequently more, and eventually owned the whole site of Bordentown. He was thus possessed of very considerable means, and founded and named the town of Bordentown. His wife died March 11, 1744–5, in her 58th year. He died September 22, 1765, leaving one son and six daughters. His will is recorded in the office of the Secretary of State at Trenton, N. J. His son—

Colonel JOSEPH BORDEN, born August 1, 1719, was a patriot of the Revolution. He was a member of the Stamp Act Congress of 1765 ; a member of the first New Jersey Convention at New Brunswick, July 2, 1774; one of the Committee of Observation of Burlington county, February, 1773; entered the army as Colonel of the 1st New Jersey Regiment, and became Colonel and Quartermaster of the State troops ; Judge of the Court of Common Pleas, September 11, 1776 ; reappointed September 28, 1781. He was a man of note in his locality, and during the war his fine house was burned by the British.[3] He was married September 22, 1743, to Elizabeth Rogers,[4] who was born at Allentown, July 10, 1725;

---

[1] *Gen. Dict.* of R. I. gives the year wrongly, 1670.

[2] According to the Borden Record, Savage is wrong in giving this date 1651.

[3] *Penn. Mag.*, ix., 435.

[4] From Robert McKean's family Bible, in possession of Mrs. Ann McKean Kerr, which is verified (as to this name) by the will of Mrs. Rogers, recorded

(daughter[1] of Samuel and Mary Rogers. An old pedigree on a modern sheet of legal foolscap, found between the leaves of the old Borden Record above quoted, states that Samuel Rogers was born 1692, died September 17, 1756; his wife, born 1690, died April 14, 1738, and verifies the dates of the daughter's birth and death here given from other sources.) Mrs. Borden died November 2, 1807. Judge Borden died April 8, 1791. His will is recorded at Trenton, N. J. His issue :[2]

i. MARY, b. July 21, 1744, married July 21, 1763, Thomas McKean, Signer of the Declaration of Independence.
ii. ANN, b. Jan. 24, 1745–6, d. June 9, 1746.
iii. ANN, b. May 9, 1747, married Sept. 1, 1768, Francis Hopkinson, Signer of the Declaration of Independence, and left issue.
iv. AMY, b. Oct. 30, 1749; d. Aug. 31, 1751.
v. LÆTITIA, b. July 29, 1751; d. June 30, 1753 N. S.
vi. JOSEPH, b. June 23, 1755; m. Nov. 26, 1778, Mary Biles, daughter of Langhorn Biles, and d. Oct. 16, 1788, leaving one child, Elizabeth, b. Nov. 13, 1779.

MINOR APPOINTMENTS.

In 1764, Mr. McKean was appointed one of the three trustees of the Loan Office of Newcastle county, for four years; which trust was renewed in 1768 and 1772 (1769, June 16[3]). This species of loan was one of the most happy expedients for the encouragement of industrious settlers in a new country, and for the improvement of lands, that was ever invented.

On the 10th of July, 1765, he was appointed by the Governor, John Penn, sole notary, and tabellion public, for the lower counties on the Delaware;[4] and in the same year was appointed justice of the peace and justice of the court of common pleas and quarter sessions, and of the orphans' court for the county of Newcastle. In the November term of 1765, and February term of 1766, he sat on the bench, and directed that all officers of the court should make use of *unstamped* paper in their several duties; and it is believed that

---

at Mt. Holly, N. J.; in which she mentions her brother Isaac Rogers. E. M. Woodward, in the *Hist. Burlington and Mercer Co.'s*, is wrong in stating that this Joseph Borden married a daughter of Marmaduke Watson. He also states wrongly the first of the family, *Benjamin* instead of *Richard*.

[1] Keith's *Provinc. Counc.*, 1883, p. 269.
[2] Robert McKean's Family Bible.
[3] *Penn. Archives*, 2d series, Wm. H. Egle, ix., 643, *et seq.*
[4] Original in possession of J. Henry Rogers, Esq., of Newcastle, Del.

this was the first court in the colonies that established such an order.

MEMBER OF THE STAMP ACT CONGRESS AT NEW YORK.

The passage of the Stamp Act in 1765 aroused a storm of indignation throughout the colonies. Had its measures been carried out, it would have been ruinous to their prosperity. "The sun of liberty is now set," said Charles Thomson, "you must light up the candles of industry and economy." To avert the threatened evils of this act, the legislature of Massachusetts proposed to the other colonies to appoint delegates to a general congress, who might consult together, and in a dutiful and loyal manner, represent the condition of affairs to the king and parliament. To this distinguished body Thomas McKean was elected a member from the three lower counties on the Delaware. His father-in-law, Col. Joseph Borden, was a member from New Jersey.[1] It met in New York, October 7, 1765, and brigadier Timothy Ruggles was elected president. James Otis, of Massachusetts, was one of the most prominent delegates, and Thomas McKean and Cæsar Rodney pillars of the cause from Delaware.[2] The congress passed a Declaration of Rights, and appointed three committees to prepare addresses to the king, the lords, and the commons; the latter committee was composed of Thomas Lynch, James Otis, and Thomas McKean.[3] The congress was dissolved on the 24th of October. A few of the members were suspected of being inimical to its designs, or of wishing to ingratiate themselves with the British ministry; and on the last day of the session, when the business was concluded, the president and three or four timid members refused to sign the proceedings. Mr. McKean then rose and addressing himself personally to the president, stated that as he had made no objections to the proceedings, he should now state his reasons for refusing to sign the petition. The president replied that he did not consider himself bound to state his objections; but upon being pressed by Mr. McKean and others for an explanation, he finally stated that "It was against his *conscience.*" Mr. McKean now rang the changes on the word *conscience* so long and loud, that a plain challenge was given and accepted in

---

[1] A list of delegates is given in Lossing's *Field Book of the Revolution,* 1860, i., 465.

[2] *Rise of the Republic,* Richard Frothingham, 1872.

[3] Ibid., and *Life of James Otis,* William Tudor, 1823.

presence of the whole congress; but the president, who, however, had no more courage to fight a duel than he had to sign the proceedings, departed from New York the next morning before dawn of day.[1] He afterwards joined the British, and fought against the colonies.[2]

Mr. Ogden, speaker of the house of Assembly of New Jersey, also refused to sign, although solicited by Mr. McKean and others in private. He at the same time desired to conceal his action from the people of New Jersey, who were zealous for the cause of America; Mr. McKean however would promise nothing more than not to mention the matter as he passed through New Jersey, unless the question was put to him. The question was asked in several different towns, and Mr. McKean stated the matter without hesitation. The speaker was burned in effigy in his town, and at the next meeting of the Assembly was removed from the office of speaker.

Upon reporting to the Assembly at Newcastle, Mr. McKean and Mr. Rodney received a unanimous vote of thanks of that house for their services.

Mr. McKean, writing to John Adams, 13th of June, 1812, mentions that he is the only survivor of the Stamp Act Congress.[3]

MINOR OFFICES.

During the next year, 1766, Mr. McKean was licensed by the governor of New Jersey, upon the recommendation of the judges of the supreme court, to practice as a solicitor in chancery, attorney-at-law and councillor, in all the courts of the province. On the 28th of October, 1769, he was appointed justice of the peace for the province of Pennsylvania, and reappointed April 10, 1773, and October 24, 1774.[4]

Of Mr. McKean's ability as a lawyer, and his ingenuity in the defense of a client, an illustration is given by a distinguished member of the Philadelphia bar, David Paul Brown, in his work, *The Forum* (ii. 339).

In a suit brought by Myers Fisher, a lawyer of note, against a person by the name of Buncom, in Chester court, for slander, in the year 1774, the defamation having been clearly made out,

---

[1] Sanderson.
[2] Lossing's *Field Book of the Revolution*, 1860, i., 465.
[3] *Adam's Works*, x., 14.
[4] *Penn. Archives*, 2d series, ix., 643 *et seq.*

Mr. McKean called some scores of witnesses, not to deny the
slander, but to show that his client was such a notorious liar
that no man in the county believed anything he said, and that
therefore no damages could possibly have been sustained by
the plaintiff. *And so the jury found.*

The early settlements upon the Delaware having been made
under the dominion of a government and courts sitting at New
York, it eventually became very inconvenient to consult the
original records; hence Mr. McKean was selected by the As-
semby in 1769, to proceed to New York, and there obtain
copies of all documents relating to real estate in the Delaware
counties, prior to the year 1700. This duty he satisfactorily
performed, and the copies thus procured were established by law
as of equal authority with the original documents.[1] In 1771
he was appointed by the commissioners of his majesty's customs,
collector of the port of Newcastle.

SPEAKER OF THE HOUSE OF ASSEMBLY.

In October 1772, Mr. McKean was unanimously elected
Speaker of the House of Assembly of Delaware. He writes
to Mr. Adams that he was unanimously elected, although only
six of the members were Whigs.[2]

The "Tea Act," so known, which went into effect a year
later, aroused more indignation than the Stamp Act. The Delaware House of Representatives referred the matter to a committee, of whom Mr. McKean was chairman. The committee
reported October 23, 1773, recommending a committee of correspondence of five members, which report was adopted, and
Colonel Rodney the speaker, George Read, Thomas McKean,
John McKinly, and Thomas Robinson, were chosen to be "A
Committee of Correspondence and Communication." On December 16th of this year, the tea was thrown overboard in
Boston.[3] When the Boston Port Bill was passed in March,
1774, closing the port of Boston, the colonies sent aid for the
sufferers in that city. The Delaware letter was signed by
Cæsar Rodney, Thomas McKean, and George Read.[4] And at a
meeting of citizens held at Newcastle, June 29, 1774, a committee of thirteen was appointed to solicit contributions for the

[1] Armor's *Lives of Governors of Penn.*, 1872.
[2] *Works of John Adams*, C. F. Adams, x., 82.
[3] Scharf's *Hist. Del.*, 1888, i., 215.
[4] Frothingham, *Rise of the Republic*, p. 387.

sufferers, among the members being Thomas McKean, George Read, and John McKinly.[1]

SECOND MARRIAGE.

About this time, Mr. McKean met with a serious affliction in the death of his wife, on Friday, the 12th of March, 1773,[2] at half-past eleven o'clock, in the 29th[3] year of her age, leaving two sons and four daughters, one of the latter being an infant two weeks old. A notice of her death appears in the *Pennsylvania Gazette* of March 17th. She was buried on the Sunday following, in the burial ground of Immanuel Church, Newcastle.[4] A crayon likeness of Mrs. McKean is in possession of Mrs. Sarah P. Wilson, of Philadelphia.

Not long after this event, either in the same year or more probably in the following year, Mr. McKean removed his residence to Philadelphia, although he also retained his house in Newcastle.

On Saturday, September 3d, 1774,[5] Mr. McKean was married a second time, to Miss Sarah Armitage, of Newcastle. They were married by the Rev. Joseph Montgomery,[6] who was, as I have ascertained, pastor of the First Presbyterian Church at Newcastle, from 1765 to 1777. No records of that church are now in existence prior to 1842.[7]

THE CONTINENTAL CONGRESS.

The political troubles of the colonies had been increasing to such an extent, that a correspondence naturally arose among the leading and influential characters throughout the continent; public meetings were held in various places, and it was finally agreed to call another general congress of the colonies to meet

[1] *Life of Geo. Read,* W. T. Read; the name wrongly spelled McKinley.

[2] Not February, 1773, as stated in *Sanderson's Lives.*

[3] Gov. McKean's Bible record, in possession of H. P. McKean, Esq.

[4] Ibid.

[5] Ibid. Not *Thursday,* as given in Sanderson. Gov. McKean's record, however, does not give the day of the week to this date.

[6] Ibid.

[7] I regret that I have been unsuccessful in finding anything about her family or history. None of the name now live in Newcastle; an old resident there tells me that he knows nothing of the name. The church records are also defective or destroyed.

in Philadelphia on the first Monday in September, 1774.[1]
The three Delaware counties met in convention, August 1,
1774, of which Mr. McKean was a member from Newcastle
county. The credentials of the Newcastle delegates were
signed by Thomas McKean, chairman of the county committee.
This convention[2] elected Cæsar Rodney, Thomas McKean and
George Read as their delegates to Congress. "Thomas Mc-
Kean," says Bancroft, "was the leading delegate from Delaware,"[3] and on the 5th of September, took his seat in this august assemblage, of which he became an invaluable ornament,
and from that day his country claimed him as her own.[4] Sanderson states that he was annually elected a member until the
first of February, 1783, and is the only member who served
from its opening until after the preliminaries of peace of 1783
were signed. He was, however, not a member during 1777.
The delegates produced their credentials and took their seats
at very irregular times, and twice the state was not represented.

The Journals of Congress (Way and Gideon, 1823), show
that the Delaware delegates took their seats as follows:

i.   1. Sept. 5, 1774. Cæsar Rodney, Thomas McKean and
           George Read are delegates at the opening of Con-
           gress.
     50-2 May 10, 1775. C. Rodney, Thomas McKean, George
           Read.
     568. Dec. 2, 1776. George Read, John Dickinson and
           John Evans. (George Read appears to have been
           rather opposed to McKean politically. In Sander-
           son's Life of Cæsar Rodney, it is stated that about
           this time the royalist party and the lukewarm in the
           lower counties contrived to come into a majority for
           a while, and one of their earliest acts was to remove
           Mr. Rodney and Mr. McKean, two delegates who
           had in every instance shown themselves the uncom-
           promising friends of liberty.")
ii.   22. Jan. 24, 1774. No delegates from Delaware. The
           President directed to inform the State.
      73. April 4, 1777. George Read, Nicholas Van Dyke,
           and James Sykes.
     368. Aug. 15, 1777. No delegates from Delaware. The
           President directed to inform the State.

---

[1] It met at Carpenter's Hall, dissolved itself in October, met May 10, 1775,
in the State House.—*Reminiscences of Carpenter's Hall.*

[2] See *Birth of the Republic,* Daniel W. Goodloe, 1889, p. 234.

[3] *Hist. U. S.,* viii. 75.

[4] *Sanderson's Lives.*

423. Jan. 30, 1778. Cæsar Rodney, Nicholas Vandyke[1] and Thomas McKean.

iii.   19. Aug. 15, 1778. Mr. McKean attended and resumed his seat.

427. Jan. 27, 1780. Mr. Vandyke produced his credentials.

581. Feb. 26, 1781. Mr. McKean attended and produced the credentials of the delegates from Delaware (names not given).

581. Feb. 27, 1781. Mr. Rodney attended and took his seat.

592. March 2, 1781. Congress reorganized under the Articles of Confederation. All the delegates' names are entered on the Journal. From Delaware, Thomas Rodney and Thomas McKean.

651. July 26, 1781. Mr. Vandyke attended.

714. Jan. 28, 1782. Mr. T. Rodney and Mr. McKean attended and took their seats.

718. Feb. 14, 1782. Mr. McKean produced the credentials of Thomas McKean, Philemon Dickinson, Cæsar Rodney and Samuel Wharton, delegates for the present year.

725. Feb. 25, 1782. Mr. Wharton attended and took his seat.

iv. 172–3. March 10, 1783. Eleazer M'Comb and Gunning Bedford appeared and produced the credentials of Cæsar Rodney, James Tilton, Eleazer M'Comb and Gunning Bedford, delegates from Delaware, elected February 1, 1783.

The term of service of Thomas McKean here ends.

On the 20th of October, 1774, Congress, as a retaliatory measure, entered into a "non-importation, non-consumption, and non-exportation agreement or association," signed by fifty-three members, including Thomas McKean and George Read, of the lower counties.[2]

Soon after taking his seat, Mr. McKean was appointed one of the committee to state the rights of the colonies, the various instances in which those rights had been violated, and the means most proper for the restoration of them; also on hearing and determining appeals in libel cases in the Court of Admiralty; besides other less important committees. He was, however, particularly useful in conducting

---

[1] A variation in spelling will be noticed.

[2] *Birth of the Republic*, D. W. Goodloe, 1889, p. 80–5. Fac similes of signatures may be found in J. J. Smith's *Am. Hist. and Lit. Curiosities*, pl. liii.

negotiations of the Secret Committee, charged with procuring arms and ammunition from abroad; and in managing the monetary affairs of the new nation; two of the most important and difficult subjects with which Congress had to deal.[1] But the most important committee of all was that appointed June 12, 1776, to prepare the Articles of Confederation between the colonies, which will be recurred to in its proper place. Of his subsequent services, it is mentioned in the papers of James Madison,[2] that Mr. McKean proposed a conditional exchange of Cornwallis for Col. H. Laurens, on condition that a general cartel should be acceded to ; and that he advocated coercion towards Vermont by moving to postpone the report of a committee in the matter, to make way for a set of resolutions, declaring Vermont in contempt of the authority of Congress, in exercising jurisdiction over certain persons professing allegiance to New York, that Vermont be required to make restitution for property taken from them, and in the event of refusal, Congress to enforce it; and, on the part of Delaware, he insisted on an equality of representation among the States.

THE COMMITTEE OF INSPECTION AND OBSERVATION, AND THE ASSOCIATORS.

In the troublous times now approaching, the people throughout the colonies elected Committees of Inspection and Observation, Committees of Correspondence, Committees of Safety, etc., and enrolled themselves in military organizations.

The Committees of Correspondence[3] were chosen during the winter of 1773–4 by the several Assemblies, upon recommendation of the House of Burgesses of Virginia. Thomas McKean was one of the Delaware Committee, as related on a previous page. The Philadelphia Committee of Inspection and Correspondence, consisting of forty-three members, was appointed June 18, 1774. A new committee of sixty-seven members for the city, and forty-two for the county, was appointed in May, 1775, but Mr. McKean's name does not appear in these lists;[4] and it is not known when he joined. This is certain, however, that he did join, for he was a member in November 1775 or

[1] Armor's *Lives of the Govs. of Penn.*
[2] Purchased by Congress, and published by Henry D. Gilpin, 1841, pp. 187–99, 200–14–20, 751–2.
[3] See Frothingham on this subject, p. 312 *et seq.*
[4] Scharf and Westcott, i, 289–92.

earlier, and subsequently became chairman. It may be con-
jectured that as Delaware was in a measure considered " the
Three Lower Counties of Pennsylvania," the Delaware Committees was merged in with the Philadelphia Committee.
There were six sub-Committees of Inspection and Observation
in Philadelphia.[1]

The Committee of Safety in Pennsylvania was constituted by
the Assembly June 30, 1775, composed of some of the most
prominent men in the colony; Henry Wynkoop, Anthony
Wayne, Edward Biddle, Thomas Willing, Benjamin Franklin,
Daniel Roberdeau, John Cadwallader, Robert Morris, Thomas
Wharton, and others, in all twenty-five, of whom seven constituted a quorum.

As early as May 1, 1775, a list was made out of persons in
the middle ward of Philadelphia, (lying west of Fourth street,
and between Market and Chestnut streets,) "able and willing to
bear arms," in which appears the name of Thomas McKean.[2]
Under this date the "roll call of Captain John Little's company, 2d battalion" gives about seventy-four names, among
whom Daniel C. Clymer is first lieutenant, and Thomas McKean
one of the privates, chiefly enrolled from the middle ward of
the city.[3]

The military organization in Pennsylvania called itself the
Associators; and being at first voluntary, became afterwards
compulsory. They were governed by a board of officers, and
a board of privates. Of the former Colonel Daniel Roberdeau
of the 2d battalion was elected president. Their Code of
Rules was approved by the Council of Safety; and soon after,
on the 8th of November, 1775, was enforced by the Assembly,
in an act enrolling all white males between the ages of sixteen
and fifty, fining those who would not bear arms. While this
bill was pending, the Quakers, a large and influential body in
Pennsylvania—a majority of whom were Tories—protested
against its passage.[4] To neutralize the effect of this, the Committee of Correspondence directed Thomas McKean, George
Clymer, Jonathan Bayard Smith, Benjamin Jones, Sharpe
Delaney, John Wilcox, and Timothy Matlack, to prepare a re-

---

[1] Scharf and Westcott, i, 290–3.

[2] *Hist. Berks and Lebanon Cos., Pa.,* I. D. Rupp, 1844, p. 401, quoting
the papers of Col. D. C. Clymer.

[3] MSS. of D. C. Clymer. See *Genealogy of the Roberdeau Family,* pp. 66,
130.

[4] *Genealogy of the Roberdeau Family,* 1876, p. 60–1.

monstrance, and with it the committee marched to the State
House.[1] The board of officers, through its chairman Colonel
Daniel Roberdeau, likewise presented a remonstrance to the
Assembly.

About May, 1776, two more battalions were added to the
Associators; the 4th, Colonel Thomas McKean, and the 5th,
Colonel Timothy Matlack, with Daniel C. Clymer as lieutenant
colonel.[2]

RESOLUTION OF THE 15TH OF MAY, AND MEETING OF MAY 20TH, 1776.

The disagreement between England and the colonies continued to increase; the king and ministry made no reply to
overtures of reconciliation that had been made by the colonies,
until at last, weary of vain efforts, Congress, on the 15th of
May passed an important act—the first of a series of events,
which culminated in the Declaration of Independence—recommending to the Colonies, that where no government sufficient
to the exigencies of their affairs had been established, to adopt
such government, and that all authority under the crown should
be suppressed, and all powers be under the authority of the
people. Some members in Congress opposed this, but Mr.
McKean was strongly in favor, and said, "that the step must
be taken, or liberty, property and life be lost."[3]

On the 23d, an address signed by William Hamilton, chairman, asked the Assembly to adhere to its instructions to the
Pennsylvania delegates in Congress against independence.
To oppose the influence of this petition, the next day the ·
Committee of Inspection and Observation came together,
with Mr. McKean as chairman, and addressed a memorial
directly to Congress, that the Assembly did not possess the
confidence of the people.[4]

"Pennsylvania was now fairly alive with the idea of independence. Nowhere had the question been more thoroughly discussed
than in its press, and nowhere was the opposition more strongly
intrenched, for it had on its side the proprietary government.
The tories could point to the instructions of the Assembly as

[1] Ibid., and Scharf and Westcott, *Hist. Phila.*, p. 302.
[2] Scharf and Westcott, p. 307, and *Penn. in War of Rev.*, W. H. Egle, 1887,
i, 556. Thos. McKean is, however, referred to as colonel as early as April
22, 1776.—*Col. Rec.*, x., 548.
[3] Bancroft, *Hist. U. S.*, 1860, viii, 368.
[4] Ibid., viii, 386-7.

the voice of one-eighth of the inhabitants of America. On this well-prepared soil fell the resolution of the fifteenth of May. The principle it embodied was accepted by the popular party as their rule of action. To give expression to the public sentiment, a great public meeting was held on the 20th of May, at the State House, which was called to order by Major John Bayard, a man of singular purity of character, brave and devout, in which Colonel Daniel Roberdeau, a gallant soldier of the Revolution, presided, and Thomas McKean, an eminent civilian, took part."[1] The resolution of the 15th of May was read and approved. A protest was drawn up, and agreed to, against the Assembly forming a new government (as that should emanate from the people). The protest was presented to the Assembly on the 22d, and laid on the table. The meeting was held in the rain, nevertheless four thousand people were present.[2] A very full account of this meeting, with the resolutions and protest, is given in Force's American Archives. (Ser. IV, vi., 517–19–845.)

This great demonstration was felt throughout the province. The position it took was responded to by local committees, public meetings, and military battalions. Following only five days after the passage of the resolution of Congress, its prompt, firm and decided action very greatly paved the way for the Declaration of Independence six weeks later.

The people having thus approved the resolution of Congress, "that all powers should be under the authority of the people," and having protested against the Assembly forming a new government, the Committee of Observation of Philadelphia, the next day, issued a call to the committees of the several counties, to send deputies to a Provincial Convention.[3] Thomas McKean, as chairman of the committee, then presented a memorial to Congress, stating that the instructions of the Pennsylvania Assembly to their delegates have a tendency to withdraw the province from its union with the other colonies, and this committee has called a meeting of all the committees of the province to take action in the matter.[4]

On the 6th of June, the 4th battalion, Colonel McKean,

---

[1] *Rise of the Republic*, Richard Frothingham. See also *Genealogy of the Roberdeau Family*, 62, and *Scharf and Westcott*, p. 312.

[2] *Scharf and Westcott*, p. 312. Also *Diary of Christopher Marshall*, William Duane, 1877.

[3] *Frothingham*, 522.

[4] Force's *American Archives*, IV., vi, 560, 689.

unanimously agreed to support the resolution of Congress of the 15th of May and the proceedings of the meeting of May 20th.[1] Other battalions likewise passed similar resolutions. In June also, on the 14th, the Delaware Assembly, at the instance of Mr. McKean, unanimously approved the resolution of Congress of the 15th of May, overturning the proprietary government within her borders.[2]

CONVENTION OF DEPUTIES AT CARPENTER'S HALL.

This important convention, which commenced on the 18th of June 1776, was the immediate result of the meeting of May 20th, and is that referred to above in the memorial of Thomas McKean to Congress. Deputies, to the number of 104, attended from all the committees in the province ; Colonel McKean, chairman of the City Committee, called the meeting to order, and stated its object. In its organization, Colonel McKean was made president, Colonel Joseph Hart, vice-president, Jonathan Bayard Smith and Samuel Cadwallader Morris, secretaries ; Benjamin Franklin, Colonel John Bayard, Timothy Matlack, and Dr. Benjamin Rush were among those present. The resolution of the 15th of May was read, and it was resolved " that the present government of the province was not competent to the exigencies of our affairs." Afterwards the convention provided for a general Provincial Convention from the whole province, to be elected by the people, to form a government for the state. This present convention in the interim seems now to have taken upon itself the general management of most of the affairs of the province ; it is appealed to to settle disputes, takes action to raise a Flying Camp; and on the 23d the chairman, Colonel McKean, Dr. Rush, and Colonel James Smith[3] are a committee to prepare a Declaration, which was agreed to on the 24th ; that the deputies are willing to concur in a vote of Congress " *declaring the united colonies free and independent states.*" The convention then adjourned, and this Declaration, signed by Thomas McKean, president, was by him delivered the next day directly to Congress.[4]

---

[1] Ibid., 784.

[2] *Bancroft*, viii., 436; *Life of George Read*, W. T. Read, 1870, p. 245; *Birth of the Republic*, Goodloe, 242.

[3] Not *Franklin*, as stated in *Sanderson's Lives.*

[4] Force's *American Archives*, IV, vi, 951–66, 1721 ; Frothingham's *Rise of the Republic*, 522–3 ; Bancroft's *History*, viii., 445 *et seq.*; Niles' *Principles and Acts of the Revolution*, 252 ; *Diary of Chr. Marshall*, Duane, p. 78 ; Scharf and Westcott, *Hist. Phil.*, 321 *et seq.*; Hickey's *Constitution*, 1853, p. 194.

THE DECLARATION OF INDEPENDENCE.

Following close upon the convention at Carpenter's Hall, and encouraged by their fearless Declaration, Congress on the 1st of July resumed the debate upon the resolution before that body which had been postponed from the 10th of June; and on the 2d of July, 1776,[1] agreed to the resolution reported from the Committee of the Whole, "That these United Colonies are, and of right, ought to be, Free and independent States. . . . ." The committee asked leave to sit again, and likewise made the same request on the 3d. On the 4th of July, 1776, the committee reported the DECLARATION to Congress, when it was unanimously agreed to.[2] There is no account of the debates on Independence: Adams spoke, as did McKean, but we have no report of what they said.[3] R. H. Lee, Wythe, Gerry, Jefferson, and Samuel Adams also gave their voices in favor.[4] " Did the able and indomitable McKean remain silent?" says Randall, in his "Life of Thomas Jefferson."[5]

When the vote was taken on the 2d of July in Committee of the Whole, Mr. McKean voted *for*, and Mr. Read *against* the resolution: the vote of Delaware was thus divided and lost (all votes being taken by States). Every State, except Pennsylvania and Delaware, had voted in favor of the measure; and it was of great importance to secure a unanimous vote. Mr. McKean, therefore, without delay dispatched an express, at his own expense, for Mr. Rodney, who was then in Delaware. That gentleman hastened to Philadelphia, and arrived at the State House, in his boots and spurs, just in time on the morning of the 4th to cast his vote in favor, and the vote of Delaware was secured. Two Pennsylvania delegates absented themselves, and that State was also united with the majority, making the vote *unanimous*.[6]

These circumstances are related by Mr. McKean in a letter to Governor Thomas Rodney, dated August 22, 1813,[7] and

---

[1] Not 1st, as stated in *Sanderson's Lives.*

[2] *Journals of Congress*, ed. 1777. See also Hickey's *Constitution*, p. 195 *et seq.*

[3] *Frothingham*, 534–7.

[4] *Historic Account of Old State House*, F. M. Etting, p. 96.

[5] I. 183.

[6] *Sanderson's Lives:* Lives of McKean and of Rodney.

[7] In possession of T. M. Rodney, Esq., pub. in fac-simile in Brotherhead's *Book of the Signers*, Phila., 1861, and also a portion, not the whole, in *Harp. Mag.*, vol. lxvii., p. 208 *et seq.*

3

again in a letter to John Adams, January 7, 1814, quoted nearly in full on a subsequent page.

Recent historians are of opinion that Mr. McKean is mistaken as to a day or two; that his patriotic and successful endeavor to bring Rodney up from Delaware, was that he might vote on the main question—the Resolution of Independence on the 2d of July.[1]

The incident just related forms the subject of a poem by the well-known writer George Alfred Townsend.[2] Thomas Mc-Kean's soliloquy, as he waits upon the State House steps for Mr. Rodney, and the concluding stanzas, are as follows:

> "Read is skulking; Dickinson is
>   With conceit and fright our foeman,
>   Wedded to his Quaker monies,"
>   Mused the grim old rebel Roman;
> "Pennsylvania, spoiled by faction,
>   Independence will not dare;
>   Maryland approves the action;
>   Shall we fail on Delaware?"
>
> In the tower the old bell rumbled,
>   Striking slowly twelve o'clock.
> Down the street a hot horse stumbled,
>   And a man in riding frock,
> With a green patch on his visage,
>   And his garments white with grime.
> "Now praise God!" McKean spoke grimly,
>   "Cæsar Rodney is on time."
>
> Silent, hand in hand together,
>   Walked they in the great square hall;
> To the roll with "Aye" responded
>   At the clerk's immortal call;
> Listened to the Declaration
>   From the steeple to the air:
> "Here this day is made a nation,
>   By the help of Delaware!"

MR. McKEAN'S SERVICES IN FAVOR OF THE DECLARATION.

Let us now briefly recapitulate Mr. McKean's services in favor of the Declaration, as above related: First, as a member of Congress, he assisted in passing the resolution of the 15th

---

[1] Mellen Chamberlain's *Authentication.*

[2] *Poetical Addresses,* Bonaventure & Co., N. Y., 1881; *Cæsar Rodney's 4th of July.*

of May. Next as an "eminent civilian," he was the chief speaker at a meeting of citizens which ratified the resolution. As chairman of the Philadelphia Committee, he issues a call for a meeting of deputies of all the committees in the State, and also reports this to Congress. As Colonel of a battalion he joins his command, and the resolution is again ratified; he takes the chair as Speaker of the Assembly of Delaware, and at his instance the resolution is again ratified; he calls to order the meeting of deputies at Carpenter's Hall, who have met together in answer to his call, and is made chairman. The meeting agrees to support a vote of Congress, that these colonies are *free and independent States*. As a privileged delegate from this meeting, he walks into Congress and lays the report before that body. He votes for the Declaration in Committee of the Whole, but his vote is neutralized by Mr. Read, who votes against him; he sends an express at his own expense for Mr. Rodney, and on the 2d, and on the memorable 4th of July, with Mr. Rodney outvotes Mr. Read, and secures a *unanimous* vote.

Had it not been for Mr. McKean's exertions, the engrossed Declaration could not have been headed as it now is—The UNANIMOUS Declaration of the Thirteen United States. Fortunate for the country was it that Mr. McKean held so many offices to give him these opportunities; and fortunate, too, that he was a man of sufficient energy and activity to make use of them to the best advantage.

THE DECLARATION OF INDEPENDENCE.—HOW SIGNED.

It is a general popular belief that the Declaration of Independence was signed on the 4th of July, 1776, as it now appears by those whose names are inseparably a part of it. The engrossed Declaration implies this, strengthened by the printed journals of Congress. The first to challenge this commonly received opinion, according to Judge Chamberlain in his *Authentication*, was Mr. McKean; and since his day many eminent writers have discussed the subject. Even the signers themselves—McKean, Jefferson and Adams, give conflicting accounts of the matter.

The question as stated by Judge Chamberlain is this: "Was the draught of the Declaration of Independence, which, after various amendments, was finally agreed to on the afternoon of July 4th, forthwith engrossed on paper, and thereupon subscribed by all the members then present except Dickinson?"

A secondary question : "Was the Declaration signed by *any one* on July 4th, 1776?" seems' to be an issue not heretofore raised by any historian ; but tacitly accepted in the affirmative as an established fact.   The author has discussed this question on a subsequent page.

Mr. McKean explicitly denies in four separate letters, that the Declaration was generally signed on July 4th : *First*, in a letter to Alexander J. Dallas, dated September 26, 1796, and published in " Sanderson's Lives ; " *secondly*, in the above mentioned letter to Governor Rodney of August 22, 1813 ; *thirdly*, in the letter to Mr. Adams of January, 1814,[1] also above mentioned — these two letters last named are almost identical, word for word, in the portions relating to this matter under discussion ; and, *fourthly*, in a letter of June 16, 1817 (eight days before his death), to William McCorkle and Son,[2] in which the letter to Mr. Dallas is largely quoted.

In the first named letter, September 26, 1796, in speaking of the printed journals, Mr. McKean says :

" By the printed publications referred to, it would appear as if the fifty-five gentlemen whose names are there printed, and none other, were on that day personally present in congress and assenting to the Declaration ; whereas the truth is otherwise. . . .

" Modesty should not rob any man of his just honor, when by that honor his modesty cannot be offended.   My name is not in the printed journals of congress as a party to the Declaration of Independence ; and this, like an error of the first concoction, has vitiated most of the subsequent publications ; and yet the fact is, that I was then a member of congress for the state of Delaware, was personally present in congress, and voted in favor of independence on the fourth of July, 1776, and signed the declaration after it had been engrossed on parchment, where my name in my own handwriting still appears.

" I do not know how the misstatement in the printed journals has happened.   The manuscript *public* journal has no names annexed to the Declaration of Independence, nor has the *secret* journal ; but it appears by the latter, that on the nineteenth day of July, 1776, the congress directed that it should be engrossed on parchment and signed by *every member*, and that it was so produced on the second of August, and *signed*.   This is interlined in the *secret* journal, in the handwriting of Charles Thomson, esquire,

---

[1] *Niles' Reg.*, July 12, 1817, xii., 305 *et seq.* ; *Adams' Works*, C. F. Adams, x., 87 ; *Mass. Hist.Col.*, 5th Ser., iv., 505, and partly quoted in Judge Chamberlain's *Authentication, Dec. Ind.*

[2] *Niles' Reg.*, xii., 278 ; Duane's *Diary of Christopher Marshall ; The Portfolio*, Sept., 1817, p. 246, quoting *Freeman's Journal*.

the secretary. The present secretary of state of the United States and myself have lately inspected the journals, and seen this."

In the letter to Mr. Adams, after speaking of other matters, Mr. McKean continues as follows:

"On the 1st July, 1776, the question was taken in the committee of the whole of Congress, when Pennsylvania, represented by seven members then present, voted against it—four to three; among the majority were Robert Morris and John Dickinson; Delaware (having only two present, namely, myself and Mr. Read) was divided; all the other states voting in favor of it. The report was delayed until the 4th; and, in the mean time, I sent an express for Cæsar Rodney to Dover, in the county of Kent in Delaware, at my private expense, whom I met at the state-house door, on the 4th of July, in his boots. He resided eighty miles from the city, and just arrived as congress met. The question was taken, Delaware voted in favor of independence; Pennsylvania (there being five members present, Messrs. Dickinson and Morris absent) voted also for it; Messrs. Willing and Humphreys were against it. Thus the thirteen states were unanimous in favor of independence. Notwithstanding this, in the printed public journal of congress for 1776, Vol. 2, it appears that the declaration of independence was declared on the 4th of July, 1776, by the gentlemen whose names are there inserted, whereas no person signed it on that day; and, among the names there inserted, one gentleman, namely, George Read, Esq,, was not in favor of it, and seven were not in Congress on that day,[1] namely, Messrs. Morris,

---

[1] Willis P. Hazard, in his edition of *Watson's Annals*, iii, 222, corrects this sentence: *Morris* should be *Messrs.*, but Hazard is still wrong. The sentence is correct, as shown by what follows: Morris was "not in Congress on that day," because he was absent, as Mr. McKean says above; the five others were not, because they had not then been elected, as he says below. In the early part of this letter, in speaking of the *vote*, Mr. McKean names Morris and Dickinson as absent; here, in speaking of the *signers*, he properly names Morris only.

After the publication of a letter of Mr. McKean in *Potter's American Monthly* (vols. iv.–v., 1875), a controversy sprang up, whether Mr. McKean should not have mentioned *nine* instead of *seven* members of Congress; but the editors as well as the contributors of that magazine are still mistaken in going back to December, 1774, for the election of delegates. A later election, November 6, 1775 (*Journals of Cong.*), returned nine members—Morton, Dickinson, Morris, Franklin, Humphreys, Biddle, Willing, Allen and Wilson. Mr. McKean mentions *seven;* the other two are Biddle, who was sick and died during the session, and Allen, a British sympathizer (*Scharf and Westcott*, i., 317). The latter abandoned his seat, June 14th, and Mr. McKean knew that two seats were permanently vacated, so that Pennsylvania was represented by *seven* only. Of the above, Morton, Morris, Franklin and Wilson signed in August; their election did not hold over, for they were re-elected July 20, 1776, together with Ross, Clymer, Rush, Smith and Taylor, nine in all, who signed in behalf of Pennsylvania. I think this matter is now clearly and correctly stated.

Rush, Clymer, Smith, Taylor and Ross, all of Pennsylvania, and Mr. Thornton of New-Hampshire; nor were the six gentlemen last named, members of congress on the 4th of July. The five for Pennsylvania were appointed delegates by the convention of that State on the 20th July, and Mr. Thornton took his seat in Congress, for the first time, on the 4th November following; when the names of Henry Wisner, of New York,[1] and Thomas McKean, of Delaware, are not printed as subscribers, though both were present in Congress on the 4th of July and voted for independence.

Here false colors are certainly hung out; there is culpability somewhere: what I have heard as an explanation is as follows: When the declaration was voted, it was ordered to be engrossed on parchment and then signed, and that a few days afterwards a resolution was entered on the secret journal that no person should have a seat in congress during that year until he should have signed the declaration of independence. . . . . After the 4th July I was not in Congress for several months, having marched with a regiment of associators as colonel, to support general Washington, until the flying camp of ten thousand men was completed. When the associators were discharged, I returned to Philadelphia, took my seat in Congress and signed my name to the Declaration on parchment. This transaction should be truly stated, and the then secret journal should be made public. In the manuscript journal, Mr. Pickering, then secretary of state, and myself saw a *printed half sheet* of paper,[2] with the names of the members afterward in the printed journals stitched in. We examined the parchment where my name is signed in my own handwriting."

Mr. McKean then turns to other subjects, and concludes:

" My sight fades very fast, though my writing may not discover it. God bless you.

Your friend,   THO'S McKEAN.
His Excellency JOHN ADAMS.

---

[1] Some authors have thought Mr. McKean was mistaken that Mr. Wisner voted for independence, because the New York delegates had not been so instructed, and since but twelve States voted on July 2d. Franklin Burdge, however, published in 1878 a memorial of Henry Wisner, quoting letters of his to show that he did vote for independence, and was the only New Yorker who so voted.

[2] There is no "*printed half-sheet* of paper" now in the journals. Mr. McKean saw the journals when Mr. Pickering was Secretary of State, 1795–1800, about seventeen years before writing this letter, and may confound the printed Declaration wafered in, with some other paper, real or imaginary, not now known.

Mr. Jefferson holds the contrary side of the question in his memoranda, as follows:[1]

" 'The Declaration thus signed on the 4th, on paper, was engrossed on parchment, and signed again on the 2d of August."

And again, in a letter of May 12, 1819, to Samuel Adams Wells:

" It was not till the 2d of July, that the Declaration itself was taken up; nor till the 4th, that it was decided, and it was signed by every member present, except Mr. Dickinson, ..."

Mr. Adams takes the same side of the question with Mr. Jefferson. In transmitting the above letter of Mr. McKean to Mercy Warren for her reading, he writes under date of Quincy, February 2, 1814:[2]

" *Dear Madam:* I send you a curiosity. Mr. McKean is mistaken in a day or two. · The final vote of independence, after the last debate, was passed on the 2d or 3d of July, and the Declaration prepared and signed on the 4th.

" What are we to think of history, when, in less than forty years, such diversities appear in the memories of living persons, who were witnesses?"

These conflicting statements should now be carefully criticised. Mr. Adams here, in his old age, contradicts what he himself said thirty-eight years before in a letter to Samuel Chase. On July 9th, five days after the passage of the Declaration, he writes: " As soon as an American seal is prepared, I conjecture that the declaration will be subscribed by all the members."[3] From which we may infer that the Declaration had not *then* been signed. The earlier letter as contemporary evidence is deserving of more credit than the later one.

As to Mr. Jefferson, Judge Chamberlain has shown in his *Authentication*, p. 8–9, that Mr. Jefferson's *Notes* were not made at the time alleged, but subsequently, and aided by the printed journals. " Hence his notes lose the authority of contemporaneous entries."

George Washington Greene says:[4] " Mr. Jefferson's memory failed him singularly in his history of that document, important as the part he bore in it was."

[1] *Jefferson's Writings*, H. A. Washington, Washington, D. C., i, 26, 120–2, vii., 124; *Randall's Life*, i., 171.

[2] *Mass. Hist. Collections*, 5th Ser., iv., 505.

[3] *Adams' Works*, ed. 1860, ix., 421; Scharf and Westcott, *Hist.*, i., 319.

[4] *Histor. View Amer. Rev.*, 379.

And after the appearance of Mrs. Morris' article on the Declaration in *Potter's American Monthly*, several others wrote expressing their opinions. Among whom, William Duane writes:[1] "Mr. Jefferson was so clearly wrong in stating that Pennsylvania's vote for Independence was secured by the appearance of new members on the fourth of July, that we have a right to suspect him in error in other points." Another writer,[2] name unknown, in an article, *The Declaration of Independence, The statements of Thomas McKean and Thomas Jefferson compared*, gives their statements in full, and says: "A gentleman of good repute, as a historical and antiquarian scholar, disagrees with Mrs. Morris, and writes us as follows: 'Mr. Jefferson, at the time he wrote his autobiography, was very old; and we all know that the memory is the first of the mental faculties to show signs of decay. He confused what was done in Congress in August, with what was done in July. He had forgotten the Mecklenburg Declaration of Independence. His account cannot be compared with the clear and positive statements of Governor Thomas McKean.'"

Mr. McKean's first statement on this subject was made twenty years after the Declaration was signed. Age had not, at this time or any other time, impaired his mental faculties; witness his subsequent vigor ten years later, while Governor of Pennsylvania, and the letter to William McCorkle and son, eight days before his death. His first statement, he reiterated during the next twenty-one years. In the main facts, his statements have not been impeached, although in some collateral matters of minor importance he may be in error.

Among recent writers, the opinion is almost unanimous that the Declaration was not generally signed on the 4th July, but was subscribed or authenticated by John Hancock president, and Charles Thomson secretary.

In his recent history, Justin Winsor[3] states distinctly that it was *signed* by the president and secretary. "The best investigators of our day are agreed that the president and secretary alone signed it on that day."

Daniel Webster,[4] Robert C. Winthrop,[5] and George Wash-

[1] Vols. iv.–v., for 1875, p. 785.
[2] Ibid., p. 651.
[3] *Narrative and Crit. History of Amer.*, 1888–9, v., 231 *et seq.*
[4] *Works*, Boston, 1872, i., 129.
[5] Oration, July 4, 1876, Boston, 1876, p. 29.

ington Greene,[1] hold that it was authenticated by the *signatures* of the president and secretary.

Peter Force,[2] the most thorough and reliable investigator of revolutionary history, George Bancroft[3] and Richard Frothingham[4] rather vaguely and perhaps cautiously state that it was *authenticated* by the president and secretary.

Benson J. Lossing formerly stated[5] that the Declaration was *signed* by the president alone, but has since changed his opinion, and has now come to the conclusion that it was *signed* by the members on the paper on which it had been written.[6]

Hildrith's History of the United States (iii, 137) and William L. Stone[7] hold that some or a few of the members *signed* on July 4th.

William T Read, in his life of his grandfather George Read (p. 229), is assuredly mistaken in saying it was *signed* on July 4th "by all present in Congress on that day except Mr. Dickinson." Force flatly contradicts this statement (originating with Jefferson) contained in Lord Mahon's History.[8]

Philadelphia's noted historian, Watson, quotes Mr. McKean's letter, that "the Declaration of Independence was not actually signed on the 4th of July."[9]

Mrs. Nellie Hess Morris, in a magazine article on the Declaration, regards it "as a question I cannot venture to decide."[10]

The latest, and most thorough and searching investigator of this subject is Judge Mellen Chamberlain, of Boston, in his *Authentication of the Declaration of Independence*,[11] wherein he shows that it was not generally signed on July 4th; but he does not touch upon any other phase of the question.

One naturally now turns to the printed journals of Congress, to see what evidence is there recorded, which can be construed so variously; but, as will be seen below, the *printed* journals are inaccurate and misleading, and have doubtless been the

---

[1] *Histor. View of Amer. Rev.*, N. Y., 1872, p. 101, 379.

[2] *The Dec. Ind., or Notes on Lord Mahon's Hist.*, London, 1855, p. 61.

[3] *Hist. U. S.*, ed. 1885, iv., 452 ; 1879, v., 332.

[4] *Rise of the Republic*, p. 544.

[5] *Field Book of Rev.*, 1860, ii., 79, and *Harp. Mag.*, xlvii., 258.

[6] *Potter's Am. Monthly*, Phila., iv.–v., for 1875, 754–7.

[7] *The Dec. of Ind. in a New Light, Harp. Mag.*, lxvii., 210.

[8] *The Dec. Ind.*, London, 1855, p. 63.

[9] *Annals*, Phila. ed., 1884, 3 vols., i., 400.

[10] *Potter's Am. Monthly*, iv.–v., 498.

[11] *Cambridge*, 1885; reprinted from *Mass. Hist. Coll.*, November, 1884.

cause of much of this confusion. The journal (for 1776) was first printed by order of Congress by Robert Aitken, Philadelphia, 1777 (vols. 1 and 2). The whole Journal is in thirteen volumes, printed from time to time by Aitken, D. C. Claypoole, John Dunlap, and J. Patterson.

The Journal was reprinted in 1777, vols. 1 and 2 only ; again in 1800 by Folwell in thirteen volumes ; and in 1823 by Way and Gideon in 4 vols. These are all the earlier editions mentioned in B. P. Poore's Catalogue of Government Publications.

The proceedings of July 4th, 1776, according to the printed Journal, 1st edition (1777), are as follows *literatim*:

"Agreeable to the order of the day, the Congress resolved itself, into a committee of the whole, to take into their farther consideration the declaration, and after some time the president resumed the chair, and Mr. Harrison reported, that the committee have agreed to a declaration which they desired him to report.

"The declaration being read, was agreed to, as follows ;

"A DECLARATION by the Representatives of the UNITED STATES of AMERICA in Congress assembled.

[*Here follows the Declaration.*]

"The foregoing declaration was by order of Congress engrossed and signed by the following members:

[*Here follow the names in groups, against the names of their respective States.*]

Resolved, That copies of the declaration be sent to the several assemblies, conventions and committees, or councils of safety, and to the several commanding officers of the continental troops ; that it be proclaimed in each of the United States, and at the head of the army."

In the editions of 1777 and 1800 there are printed but fifty-five names subscribed—Mr. McKean's being omitted. In the later edition of 1823 this omission is corrected, and his name is printed with the others. The discovery of this omission of Mr. McKean's name (and which will be referred to more fully under the signing of the Declaration on parchment,) was one of the causes which led to this discussion as to the signing.

Wishing to settle the matter if possible, I obtained permission from the Secretary of State to examine the original manuscript journals of Congress. After a perusal of them, I came into possession (through the kindness of the author,) of Judge Mellen Chamberlain's *Authentication of the Declaration of*

Thursday July 4. 1776

July 4

Resolved That an application be made to the committee of safety of Pennsylvania for a supply of flints for the troops at New York and that the colony of Maryland and Delaware be requested to embody their militia for the flying camp with all expedition and to march them without delay to the city of Philadelphia

Agreeable to the order of the day the Congress resolved itself into a committee of the whole to take into their further consideration the declaration

The president resumed the chair

Mr Harrison reported that the committee of the whole Congress have agreed to a Declaration which he delivered in.

The Declaration being again read was agreed to as follows

IN CONGRE
A DECLAR
BY THE REPRESE
UNITED STAT
IN GENERAL CON

WHEN in the Course of human Events, it becomes...
with another, and to assume among the Powers of...
Nature's God entitle them, a decent Respect to the O...
to the Separation

We hold these Truths to be self-evident, th...
inalienable Rights, that among these...
instituted among Men, deriving their just Powers from th...
Ends, it is the Right of the People to alter or to abolish...

Independence; and found that in this investigation, I had unknowingly been pretty much treading in his footsteps.

It may be explained here, that there are *three* original manuscript journals, which are almost wholly in the handwriting of Charles Thomson: 1st. The Rough Journal, so called, consisting of entries made probably while Congress was sitting, which is the standard. 2d. The Smooth Journal, a copy of the previous, the entries being somewhat amplified and punctuated. The 3d is the Secret Journal, which is not a daily record, the consecutive dates of a portion in 1776 being June 24; July 8, 11, 17, 19; August 2; then November 27. There is consequently in the Secret Journal no entry under July 4, 1776.

In the manuscript Smooth Journal, the declaration is wholly in writing, with no attesting clause, and no names attached, either in writing or in print.

Upon examining the Rough Journal, much to my surprise, I found no *written* names appended to the Declaration, not even Hancock's, and the Declaration itself, with the attestation, is *in print* on a large folded sheet of paper, attached by four red wafers. These facts do not appear to have been generally known, or at least have not appeared in print, before the publication of Judge Chamberlain's pamphlet.

The page of the journal of July 4th is towards the left hand, and is 12¼ by 8 inches with a margin of 2½ inches, on the edge of the page at the left, not separated by any line. In the margin is a duplicate date, and in the body of the page the writing covers slightly more than half of the page; the lower part being left blank, undoubtedly to receive the printed broadside now found there. This page of the journal is here reproduced in fac-simile, a photo-lithograph, and reduced one-half size of the original. For this especial favor,—the first time that any portions of these journals have been reproduced in fac-simile,—the author is indebted to the Hon. William F. Wharton, Assistant Secretary of State, and to Frederick Bancroft, Esq., Chief of the Bureau of Rolls and Library.

The Declaration is on paper 18 inches long by 14¾ inches wide; the print covering a space 17⅜ by 11¾ inches. It is folded upwards at the bottom of the page (where it is at the present time worn away and torn completely across,) and folded a second time in closing the book. It begins and ends as follows, the positions of the wafers being also shown:

O O   O
          In CONGRESS, July 4, 1776.
O A DECLARATION
          By the REPRESENTATIVES of the
UNITED STATES OF AMERICA,
          In GENERAL CONGRESS assembled.

WHEN in the courſe of human events, it becomes necefsary

[*Here follows the Declaration*]

Signed by ORDER and in BEHALF of the CONGRESS,
          JOHN HANCOCK, President.
ATTEST.
CHARLES THOMSON, Secretary.

PHILADELPHIA: PRINTED BY JOHN DUNLAP.

Lossing states that the Declaration was passed about two
o'clock.[1] It was printed during the day and evening ; and the
next day sent forth to the world.[2]   On the 8th, by order of
the Committee of Safety, it was publicly read by John Nixon
from the State House steps. In Judge Chamberlain's *Authentication*, a letter from Theodore F. Dwight, librarian of the
State Department, states that this first publication is the one
wafered in the journal, and that among the papers of Washington is another copy, the same which he read, or caused to be
read, to the army.

The Declaration was also published in the *Evening Post* of
of July 6th, signed by the President and Secretary, and later
it appeared in other papers.

The reader has now before him all the facts upon which the
foregoing diversified opinions are based. It is seen that there
is no copy of the Declaration signed in the *handwriting* of
any one on July 4th, the only attestation being in *print* ; and
no paper is known such as mentioned by Jefferson, signed by
all the members. It cannot be denied that such a paper ever
existed, for "it may have lost," says Judge Chamberlain,

[1] *Field Book*, 1860, ii., 78.
[2] Scharf and Westcott, i., 317 ; Frothingham, 544.

"but there are facts making it far more probable that it never existed."[1]

The responsibility of inserting the names in the printed journal cannot now be determined, and it is reasonable to suppose that there was no intention to mislead. The Secret Journal had not then been printed; and since the only entry as to the engrossing and signing of the Declaration is contained in it, the names were probably inserted in the public journal for the information of the public.[2] It is unfortunate, for it makes the printed journal assert facts on July 4th which did not take place until August or later.

Since there is no Declaration known, in or out of the journals of Congress, containing the *written* signatures of the president and secretary affixed on the 4th of July, and not a scrap of evidence that such a paper ever existed, the author considers it very doubtful whether even Hancock or Thomson signed on the 4th.

In the first place it was not the custom of the Continental Congress that resolutions in general should be *signed* by any one. When passed, they were entered on the journal. Subsequently, copies of resolutions that were sent to General Washington and others, were authenticated by the written signature of John Hancock; but such papers were *copies*, and not original records. There are no *signed resolutions* among the miscellaneous papers of Congress preserved by Charles Thomson. This volume of papers was shown to me when making inquiries at the Department of State, where the facts in this paragraph were ascertained. In answer to a further inquiry as to whether there are any resolutions of the Continental Congress signed in writing by the President, or by the President and Secretary, the following letter states the matter officially:

DEPARTMENT OF STATE,
WASHINGTON, October 21, 1889.

ROBERDEAU BUCHANAN, ESQR.,
The Clarendon, Washington City.

Sir: In reply to the enquiry contained in your letter of the 3d instant, I have to say that there are not in the Archives of the Continental Congress in this Department any resolutions or other papers signed *in writing* by the President or by the President and Secretary prior to their entry on the journals.

I am, sir, your obedient servant,
J. FENNER LEE, *Chief Clerk.*

---

[1] *Authentication*, p. 15.
[2] Ibid., p. 20, Letter of T. F. Dwight.

Is it likely that John Hancock would violate the usual custom of Congress by signing the Declaration unless especially
authorized to do so? And the question may also be asked:
If it required a formal resolution to prepare and sign the engrossed Declaration on the 2d of August, would it not likewise
have required a similar resolution for Hancock to sign the
Declaration on the 4th of July? No such resolution appears
on the journal, and we may therefore doubt such alleged signing. In accordance with custom, the entry on the journal is
a sufficient attestation of the *fact* that the Declaration had
passed Congress.

No argument can be drawn from the wording of the attesting clause—*Signed by order and in behalf of*—that it presup-
poses a resolution of Congress; because these words, and others
of similar import, have several times been made use of in other
documents, showing the phrase to be one of common use in
those days, but perhaps obsolete at the present time.[1]

As no Declaration bearing the written *signature* of John
Hancock on July 4th is known ever to have been in existence,
we have only the *printed* Declaration from which to infer the
signing. This signing, if it was done, was not the vital act,
giving life and force to the Declaration; but merely the attestation of that act already consummated; and, judging by the
printed broadside, performed wholly for the satisfaction of the
public. It was therefore a matter of secondary importance.
This written copy itself was not intended to go before the public, or to be used in any legal proceeding; it was simply a
printer's copy, and the printed Declaration made from it would
be the same whether printed from genuine signatures or from
the same names written by another person. And from these
considerations, the author hazards the conjecture that *no one
properly signed on July 4th*. But in preparing a copy of the

---

[1] In support of this statement, the following may be found in Force's
American Archives: IV., vi., 1136, Address to Gen. Washington, June 29,
1776, "By desire, and in behalf of the several Regiments in the Second
Brigade;" IV., vi., 847, Petition of Gen. Daniel Roberdeau to the Assembly,
May 20, 1776, "Signed in behalf of, and by the desire of the inhabitants,"
etc.; V., i., 170, Address to Gen. Roberdeau, July 10, 1776, "Signed by order and in behalf of the Battalion;" V., ii., 1075, Address of inhabitants of
New Jersey to Governor Tryon, October 16, 1776, "Signed by desire and
in behalf of the inhabitants;" V., iii., 484, Address by a meeting of citizens,
November 2, 1776, "Signed by order and in behalf of, the meeting." These
were found by casually turning over the pages of Force's *Archives ;* doubtless there are others. See also *Genealogy of the Roberdeau Family*, pp. 61,
62, 63, 68. This same wording much amplified is also made use of in the
Articles of Confederation.

Declaration for the printer, some one,—perhaps Charles Thomson, used the customary attesting phrase, and wrote his own name as secretary, and that of John Hancock as president. And this paper being no part of the public records was not preserved. Thus these two names might have appeared in print, with no manuscript as their authority, to turn up at a later day for the satisfaction of investigators.

This view presented itself to me upon reading the broad expression *authenticated*, made use of by George Bancroft and others, as though they did not feel warranted by the facts to employ the unequivocal word *signed*. Hancock could "authenticate" the Declaration by directing Charles Thomson to write his name for him in the printer's copy, although that act would not be *signing*.

This opinion is admitted to be a mere inference, but it is a simple inference, and a natural one to be drawn when there is no evidence. It stands upon grounds certainly as firm as the opposite side of the question, which is based upon a complex inference; that because there are printed signatures there must have been written ones. The simple and plain inference here is, that because there are printed signatures there may have been *written names;* but to go farther, and infer again that those written names were *genuine signatures*, is a double inference not warranted.

Considered under the theory of probabilities, if we assume the chances to be equal, whether there were written names or not, the probability that there were, is $\frac{1}{2}$. And if the chances are equal that the written names were signatures, the probability of this being so, is $\frac{1}{2}$ of $\frac{1}{2}$, or $\frac{1}{4}$. The probability that they were *not* signatures, is also $\frac{1}{4}$ (because we suppose the chances to be the same), and these two fourths together make up the half first obtained. Suppose now, to further illustrate this, we make a new condition, and ask, whether the names were written with a pen or a pencil; if one is just as likely to occur as the other, the probability is $\frac{1}{2}$ of $\frac{1}{2}$ of $\frac{1}{2}$, or $\frac{1}{8}$.

We see, therefore, that like a pair of scales, there is a balance kept up; the more we weigh down one side with conditions the higher does the other side ascend, and the lighter or less is the probability of the occurrence. The *degree* of probability may be different in each step, but the reasoning will be the same; for example, the probability of there having been written names may be greater than $\frac{1}{2}$; and persons may differ in their estimates of these quantities. However they may be varied, the more steps we take from known facts the less the probability; the probability of the first step (that there were written names) must necessarily be greater than the second step (that these names are genuine signatures), because the latter is represented by the product of two proper fractions, which product must necessarily be less than either fraction. The second step *may* equal, but can never exceed the former in probability. Therefore we conclude that it is more probable that there were written names, than that they were genuine signatures.

Another aspect of the question is this: It being a legal maxim that it is impossible to prove a negative, the burden of proof is thrown upon those who hold the affirmative of any question to bring forward evidence to support it; and that has not been done in this case, for an inference is not proof; therefore the negative side of this question should stand until overthrown by some evidence; and we must hold that the names were not genuine signatures.

Why it is, that in preference to this simple negative inference, the far-fetched affirmative side should be generally held, can easily be explained if we examine the facts as they successively became known. The copies of the Declaration sent to the States, the published journals of Congress, and the engrossed Declaration itself, all point to the 4th of July as the date of the general signing. Mr. McKean alone held the correct opinion, and he was contradicted by Jefferson and Adams. This opinion generally obtained for forty-five years, until the Secret Journals were published in 1821. So strong a hold has it taken upon the public mind, that like many popular fallacies it has gained the impress of truth. It is still held by the vast majority of people, and doubtless will also be till the end of time. When the Secret Journals were published, and it was found that the general signing did not take place on July 4th, this popular idea of *signing*, still holding possession of the minds of investigators, warped their judgment; and imbued with the idea that *somebody* signed on the 4th, if not the fifty-six, they naturally turned to the first printed copies of the Declaration, and from them inferred that John Hancock and Charles Thomson were those who *signed* on that day.

The main question having now been considered in the light of the custom of Congress, demonstrated by mathematics, judged by legal maxims, and examined with our minds not warped by pre-conceived notions, we are constrained to the

of that lake and report the result of their enquiry as soon as possible to Congress.

July 17. 1776

Resolved That the committee appointed on the 10th of this month "to make strict enquiry" be directed to apply to the Convention of Pensylvania now sitting and request them to appoint a select committee of their body to confer with them on a matter of importance relating to that state

July 19. 1776

Resolved That the Declaration passed on the 4th be fairly engrossed

Resolved That the secret committee be empowered to contract with Mr Mease for the importation of goods to the amount of thirty thousand pounds sterling at their risque and fifteen thousand pounds sterling at the risque of the United States of America for the public service.

That the marine committee be empowered to purchase a swift sailing vessel to be employed by the secret committee in importing said goods.

November 27. 1776

Resolved That a committee of three be appointed to procure a translation into the german language of the treaty between the court of London & Hesse for troops to be employed in America: That the said committee be fully authorised to pursue means the most effectual in their judgment for communicating to the Hessians the said treaties and

Aug 2 — Engrossed on parchment with the title and stile of "The unanimous declaration of the 13 united States of America" and that the same when engrossed be signed by every member of Congress.

NP Aug 2. 1776. The declaration of independence being engrossed & compared at the table was signed by the members.

conclusion that no one properly signed the Declaration of Independence on July 4th, 1776.

THE ENGROSSED DECLARATION.

As to the signing of the Declaration on parchment there is no uncertainty. The record is contained in the Secret Journal, first published by order of Congress by Thomas B. Wait in 1821. In this publication the record stands as follows, *literatim*:

"July 19, 1776. Resolved, That the declaration passed on the 4th be fairly engrossed on parchment, with the title and style of —'THE UNANIMOUS DECLARATION OF THE THIRTEEN UNITED STATES OF AMERICA;' and that the same, when engrossed, be signed by every member of Congress."

"August 2, 1776. The Declaration of Independence being engrossed, and compared at the table, was signed by the members."[1]

This page of the original manuscript Secret Journal is 12¼ by 7¾ inches, ruled with a red line forming a margin of 1⅛ inches on the left side. The whole entry is seen to be a post entry, and interlined. It is in ink decidedly lighter colored than the rest of the page. This page reduced one-half size, is also here reproduced as a photolithograph.[2] For this privilege we are indebted, as in the former case, to the Hon. William F. Wharton, Assistant Secretary of State, and to Frederick Bancroft, Esq., Chief of the Bureau of Rolls and Library.

In accordance with the vote of Congress, the engrossed Declaration was signed on the 2d of August by the fifty-four members then present; Mr. McKean and Thornton signed later, making the fifty-six. This document is now in the Department of State ; the signatures are arranged in six columns of 3, 7, 12 headed by Hancock, 12, 9 and 13 names, the delegates of each State in groups—except Hancock, the president, and Thornton who signed later — but without the names of the States (which are improperly printed in the published journals). Mr. McKean's name is the last in the fourth column, with the names of the other delegates from Delaware.

It is related that Hancock, the president, as he affixed his huge signature, exclaimed, "'There! John Bull can read my

---

[1] See also Force's *American Archives*, V., i., 1584–97.

[2] This is the first time that any portion of these Journals has been literally reproduced in fac-simile, although portions have been very accurately printed by Judge Chamberlain from the letter of Theodore F. Dwight. The word *Declaration*, line 2 of proceedings of July 4th (*Authentication*, p. 18, l. 17), should commence with a capital.

5

name without spectacles, and may double the reward of £500 for my head. *That* is my defiance."[1] Dickinson, who opposed the Declaration, said, "We are not ripe," to whom Witherspoon replied : "Not ripe, sir! In my judgment we are not only ripe, but rotting. Almost every colony has dropped from its parent stem, and your compromise, sir, needs no sunshine to mature it.[2] "There go a few millions," said one, as Carroll, of Carrollton, the wealthiest member, attached his name. "We must all hang together now," remarked Hancock; "Yes," replied Franklin, "or else we shall hang separately."

There were in Congress on the 4th of July, 1776, seventy members, of whom about fifty-one were in their seats. Some of these seventy afterwards joined the British, and the terms of others expired before the 2d of August, so that on that day only forty-seven of these seventy signed, Mr. McKean, the 48th, was the last of all to sign. During the interval, however, seven new members were elected as follows: Rush, Ross, Clymer, J. Smith, and Taylor, all of Pennsylvania; Carroll and Chase, of Maryland. Besides these, Thornton of New Hampshire was subsequently elected, and took his seat November 4th. He also received permission to sign, making up the fifty-six names.[3]

Immediately after the passage of the Declaration on the 4th of July, Mr. McKean obtained leave of absence to march with his battalion, and was not present when the engrossed copy was signed August 2d. As late as August 8th, 1776, Cæsar Rodney writes to Thomas Rodney that Mr. McKean is still in the Jerseys, and not likely soon to return.[4] On the 27th of August Mr. McKean was present at the opening of the Delaware Constitutional Convention at Newcastle.[5] And according to Mr. McKean's letter to Thomas Rodney above mentioned, and quoted on a subsequent page, and also the letters to Mr. Adams on a previous page, it would appear that he signed the Declaration between these two dates, and not as late as October, as stated in "Sanderson's Lives."

There are circumstances, however, which render this inference doubtful. Congress, on January 18th, 1777, directed that copies of the Declaration, with the names then subscribed, should be authenticated and sent to each State. The names

[1] Watson's *Annals*, 1884, i., 399.
[2] Lossing, *Harp. Mag.*, iii., 155.
[3] Scharf and Westcott, i., 317 *et seq.*
[4] Force, *Am. Archives*, V., i., 833.
[5] Journal, pub. 1776.

were then accordingly printed for the first time,[1] and these
copies were transmitted to the States by Hancock about January 31, 1777. Mr. McKean's name does not appear upon
these copies, although Thornton's name is there ; from which
it seems evident that Mr. McKean did not sign until after January 18th or 31st, 1777. William L. Stone, in his article,
The Declaration of Independence in a New Light,[2] says,
" Thomas McKean from Delaware, as he says himself, did not
sign till January, 1777." Bancroft states in his History,[3] that
Mr. McKean signed in 1781, which is in itself preposterous,
from the nature of the instrument. Peter Force, who knew
more of Revolutionary history than any man living in later days,
does not appear to have known the exact date ; he says,[4] " The
signing by the members was discontinued at the close of the year
1776. . . . . . One signature only,—that of Thomas McKean
—was afterwards added to the Declaration of Independence."

Mr. McKean in the letter to Mr. Adams, already quoted,
says, "After the 4th of July I was not in Congress for several
months." He repeats this in the letter to Mr. Rodney ; but
after the Delaware convention had dissolved, September 21st,
he was probably in Congress on the 25th and 27th, for on
those days he was appointed on certain committees. His name
does not appear again in the journal during this year. From
December 2, 1776, to January 30, 1778, he was not a member
of Congress, though he was undoubtedly in Philadelphia or
wherever Congress was in session during that time, and might
have signed during this interval.

In the earlier publications of the Journals of Congress, as
already remarked, Mr. McKean's name was omitted from the
list of signers of the Declaration. " The error," says he, in
the letter to William McCorkle and Son, June 16, 1817,[5] remained uncorrected until 1781,[6] when I was appointed to print
the laws of Pennsylvania." In 1796, Alexander J. Dallas,
also in printing the laws of Pennsylvania, discovered the dis-

---

[1] Journals; also Winsor s *Nar. and Crit. Hist.*, vi., 268.

[2] *Harp. Mag.*, lxvii., 211. Mr. Stone kindly informs the author that he
gathers this statement only from Mr. McKean's four letters on this subject.

[3] Ed. 1886, ix., 60 ; ed. 1885, v., 16. Justin Winsor, in his *History*, vi.,
268, and Judge Chamberlain, in his *Authentication*, p. 21, as collateral matter have quoted this date of Bancroft's.

[4] *The Dec. Ind.*, etc., London, 1855, p. 65.

[5] *Niles' Reg.*, xii., 278, and *Diary of Christopher Marshall*, Duane, 1877, p.
291 *et seq.*

[6] This expression and date may have misled Mr. Bancroft.

crepancy and investigated it. Mr. McKean's reply to Mr.
Dallas, dated September 26, 1796, gives this explanation:
"The journal was first printed by Mr. John Dunlap in 1778,[1]
and probably copies, with the names then signed to it, were
printed in August 1776, and that Mr. Dunlap printed the
names from one of them."[2] Mr. McKean's name is omitted in
the Journals of Congress, by Aitken 1777, and by Folwell in
1800. In the copies of the Declaration sent to the several
states by Congress in January 1777;[3] and in *The Constitutions of the Several States,* William Jackson, London, 1783,
and in the Laws of Delaware, 1797, [by George Reed].
His name first appeared with those of the other signers, in
McKean's Laws 1782, which he had been appointed to publish
in 1781; also in *Dallas' Laws,* 1797; in *The Constitutions of the United States,* William Duane, 1806; in the
published Journals of the Pennsylvania Senate, December 2,
1807, under an order that the Declaration be read and inserted
in the Journal; (This copy is peculiar, by reason of its having
the name of Charles Thomson inserted under that of John
Hancock, and before the names of the other signers.) In
Tyler's fac simile of the Declaration 1818; *Journals of Congress,* Way and Gideon, 1823, and probably in all subsequent
publications of the Declaration.

Of early official printed copies of the Declaration, the first
was that of Dunlap, July 4–5, 1776; the next was by Mary
Katharine Goddard in Baltimore, which is the publication at-
tested by Hancock and Thomson, in their own hands, and sent
to the States.[4]

Of fac-similes, the earliest was that of Benjamin Owen Tyler,
styling himself "professor of penmanship," in 1818; it is in
Italian script with fac similes of signatures, and certified to,
by Richard Rush, acting Secretary of State.[5] This has been
engraved on copper and published on vellum, and on paper. A
fac-simile is published in Force's American Archives, 1848,
V. i, 1597, bearing the imprint "W. J. Stone, Sc. Washn."
One was published in New York in 1865; and another in *The*

[1] John Dunlap printed some of the later volumes, and Mr. McKean, without looking in the earlier volumes, may have assumed that Dunlap printed
them all.

[2] *Sanderson,* where the letter is given in full.

[3] One of these has found its way to the Boston Public Library; a copy of
another is given in *Hist. Mag.,* Notes and Queries, IV., 2d Ser., Nov., 1868.

[4] Winsor's *Hist.,* vi., 268.

[5] A copy is in the State House at Annapolis.

Declaration of Independence, Boston, 1876.[1] A photolithograph, half size, by N. Peters, Washington, D. C., in 1873,
certified by C. Delano, Secretary of the Interior, and M. D.
Leggett, Commissioner of Patents. Another by A. G. Gedney, Washington, 1883, photographed, half size, from the
original parchment: below this are fac-simile of the signatures
with the imprint—"Restoration of signatures, from a copper
plate engraving in fac-simile, made by order of President
Monroe in 1823."[2] Fac similes of the signatures alone, are
given in Lossing's *Field Book of the Revolution*, 1860, pp.
80–1; in Winsor's *History* already quoted, vi., 263–6;
Harper's Magazine, iii., 158–9; and in numerous other works.

The family of Commodore McKean, in Binghamton, N. Y.,
is in possession of what is probably a fac simile of the Declaration on parchment. The author not having seen it is unable
to identify it with such as have been described.

It is unfortunate that at the present day the signatures can
with difficulty be made out on the engrossed Declaration, which
is in the State Department. A recent writer has said that the
ink was *stolen!* that some one obtained permission to make a
fac simile of the Declaration, and passed the parchment between
heavy rollers which took up most of the ink, causing the writing to become faint, and many of the signatures wholly illegible.

WAR MEASURES.

On the day the Declaration was passed, Congress resolved
that the delegates in Congress from New York, New Jersey,
and Pennsylvania, the Council of Safety, the Committee on Observation and Inspection for Philadelphia, and the field officers
of the Pennsylvania battalions, should be a committee to take
measures for the safety of New Jersey. This committee met
the next day, the 5th, and Colonel McKean was called to the
chair. It was ordered that all the military march without delay
to Trenton, except three battalions which go to New Brunswick.[3]

In consequence of the above order, Colonel McKean marched
at the head of his battalion to Perth Amboy,[4] in New Jersey, to

---

[1] Winsor's *Hist.*, vi., 266.

[2] While this page is in press, Mr. Gedney states that this copper plate
is the one bearing the imprint of W. J. Stone, and the same which caused
the ruin of the parchment Declaration; that a damp paper was placed over
the signatures to transfer them, blotting out nearly all the writing.

[3] Force, *American Archives*, Ser. V., i., 14 *et seq.*

[4] See also *Historic Mansions of Phil.*, Thompson Westcott, p. 488.

support General Washington. The Pennsylvania Associators were under command of General Daniel Roberdeau, who had been elected to the command of the Pennsylvania militia.[1] A letter from Colonel McKean, published in *Sanderson's Lives*, gives an account of his battalion being under fire. After the flying camp of 10,000 men had been completed, the Associators were relieved. In the Pennsylvania *Evening Post* of August 13, 1776, is published a resolution of the convention for the State of Pennsylvania, that such battalions as shall furnish their quota of the flying camp, may return home if the generals and field officers shall judge it to be expedient. And about this time Colonel McKean returned to his seat in Congress, and perhaps at that time signed the engrossed Declaration, as already related.

PUBLIC MEETINGS.

A new Constitution for the State, proposed by Franklin, was considered in a public meeting at the State House, October 21, at which Colonel John Bayard was chairman; about 1500 persons attended. The Constitution proposed was generally objectionable on account of certain religious qualifications, as well as for various other reasons. Thomas McKean, John Dickinson and others, opposed it; James Cannon, Timothy Matlack, Dr. Young, and Col. James Smith, favored it.[2]

Not long after this, November 25, 1776, Mr. McKean presided at a meeting at the Indian Queen,[3] to counteract the influence of the Tories. It appears that they were in the habit of meeting at taverns, and singing *God save the King*.[4] These trifles show the earnestness of Mr. McKean, and the great interest he had in the cause of independence. Although filling the exalted position of a delegate in Congress, he deemed nothing too insignificant to receive his aid, when it led towards independence. He endured the privations of a soldier's life, speaks at one meeting, presides at another, meets with the Council of Safety, presides at the Delaware Assembly, and we next find him in quite another sphere.

---

[1] Elected at Lancaster, Pa., July 4th, 1776, by representatives of the 57 battalions in the State. Thomas McKean was one of the candidates voted for, and received a few votes. (*Genealogy of the Roberdeau Family*, p. 67.)

[2] Scharf and Westcott, i., 324; *Diary of Christopher Marshall*, Duane, p. 98.

[3] Described in *Pa. Mag.*, xi., 103, 503.

[4] Scharf and Westcott, i., p. 326.

WRITES THE CONSTITUTION FOR THE STATE OF DELAWARE.

During his absence in the army, Colonel McKean was elected a member of the convention for forming a constitution for the state of Delaware. No sooner had he resumed his seat in congress, than his attendance was required at New-castle[1] as a member of this convention. He reached that place in a single day. Immediately upon his arrival, after a fatigu-ing ride, he was waited upon by a committee of gentlemen, members of the convention, who requested that he would pre-pare the constitution for them. He retired to his room at the public inn, sat up all night, and wrote that constitution *with-out the aid of a book or the least assistance.* At ten o'clock the next morning, it was presented to the convention, by whom it was unanimously adopted.[2] Understanding the wants and feelings of the people, well versed in law and the principles of republicanism, and a ready writer, he was able to perform in a few hours, a work that in modern times requires the labors of an expensive assembly for months.[3]

Mr. McKean relates this remarkable incident in the letter to Governor Rodney, dated August 22, 1813, already alluded to as published in *fac-simile,* in Brotherhead's *Book of the Signers;* the paragraph is as follows:

"When the associators were discharged I returned to Phila-delphia, took my seat in Congress, and signed the declaration on parchment. Two days after I went to Newcastle, joined the Convention for forming a constitution for the future government of the State of Delaware (having been elected a member for Newcastle county,) which I wrote in a tavern without a book or any assistance."

This has been justly regarded as the greatest act of Mr. Mc-Kean's life; requiring not only a profound knowledge of law and politics, but a quick perception, a good memory, clear dis-criminating judgment, and a ready pen, to accomplish so much in so short a time. It will be remembered that this was mainly original work, there being few or none other constitu-tions in those days to serve as a guide. This constitution may be seen in *The Federal and State Constitutions*, B. P. Poore, 1877.

---

[1] Sanderson and others give this wrongly, *Dover;* Mr. McKean states it correctly in his letter quoted below.

[2] Sanderson, Goodrich and other biographies.

[3] Judson's *Lives.*

Mr. McKean's claim to be the author of this constitution has been disputed in favor of George Read, and although the counter-claim rests upon very untenable grounds, yet it would not be quite fair to wholly ignore it in this biography. Fifty-seven years after Mr. McKean wrote the statement just quoted, William T. Read, Esq., claimed that his grandfather wrote the constitution, because a copy was found in that gentleman's handwriting—a very untenable argument, for he *may* have copied it. Such a writing might be used in corroboration to strengthen other evidence; but it has no force as evidence when used alone. The statement in full is as follows:

"Among Mr. Read's papers I find a document in his handwriting indorsed 'Original Draft of the System of Government of the Delaware State, with Amendments,' which makes it certain that he wrote this first constitution of Delaware." [1]

Not quite so certain, for the very caption of this paper is fatal to such claim. This heading,—-Original Draft, etc., *with amendments* never could have been written until *after* the amendments had been proposed ; that is, long after the original draft had been submitted to the convention ; consequently this paper in Mr. Read's handwriting can not be that *original* draft of the constitution. The true original draft would not have been entitled the draft *with amendments*.

Mr. Read, so far as we know, did not claim this honor for himself ; nor is any mention made of such claim in his biography in " Sanderson's Lives," written by William T. Read.[2] It first appears in Allibone's Dictionary of Authors, in 1854, by whom written is unknown, but presumed to be by William T. Read, who was a member of the Delaware Historical Society, and therefore a very likely person to have supplied this biography to Dr. Allibone. And it was not until 1870, nearly sixty years after Mr. McKean's Rodney letter was written, that the grounds for the claim were made public. Why such delay in making known a historical matter, if Mr. Read really were the author ?

In a note to the passage above cited, William T. Read then attacks Mr. McKean's statement. After quoting the paragraph upon this question in " Sanderson's Lives," he alludes to it as " this fine specimen of glorification," notwithstanding the fact that he has just made a similar claim in behalf of his own grandfather. Whether this latter should also be considered a fine

[1] *Life and Corresp. Geo. Read*, William T. Read, 1870, p. 186.
Ibid., p. 159, authorship so stated.

specimen of glorification, he has apparently left to the judgment of the reader. However this may be, Mr. Read then goes on further to criticise the several statements in "Sanderson's Lives," that the convention was held at *Dover* (which should be *Newcastle*), that Mr. McKean *himself* presented the constitution to the convention, and that it was adopted the *next morning*. Although these criticisms are just, yet the mistakes are not Mr. McKean's, but Sanderson's, caused by amplifying Mr. McKean's simple statement, "which I wrote in a tavern without a book or any assistance." In attacking collateral statements, Mr. Read seems to overlook the fact that the main question still stands uncontradicted.

It seems to be more than anything else, either carelessness or an error of judgment on Mr. Read's part to advance this claim for his grandfather; since he has neither refuted Mr. McKean's claims, nor substantiated a claim for George Read.[1]

Mr. McKean's character for integrity is sufficiently well established by his acts, and fully made known by the concurrent testimony of impartial historians, to warrant the statement that if Mr. McKean says he wrote that constitution, *it is so*. Lossing, the historian, in his *Biographical Sketches of the Signers* (1860, pp. 140–4), accredits Mr. McKean with the authorship, and not Mr. Read. Scharf, in his *History of Delaware* (2 vols., 1888, i., 187, 203), accredits the authorship to each in his biographical sketches, showing that he had not carefully examined the question.

George Read as president of the convention, would naturally require a copy of the constitution under discussion, so as to intelligibly direct the proceedings. The amendments on this paper being "in a different handwriting, probably that of the

---

[1] This is not the only mistake or inaccuracy in the volume. The name McKinly is spelled wrongly throughout the volume. On page 344 Mr. Read states that Mr. McKean died June 17th, and that he had *eleven* children by his second wife—both of which are wrong. Regarding this convention he has several mistakes: He says in the text, page 182, that the sub-committee reported on the 13th, the report read a second time, and re-committed on the 15th; reported again on the 16th; and in the note page 187, these dates are given 13th, 14th and 18th respectively, all of which are wrong except the second date named. Moreover, the two pages are not consistent with one another. May we not also suspect Mr. Read of carelessness elsewhere? These, however, are trifles compared with the grievous historical mistake he makes on page 229 and elsewhere, in saying that "the Declaration of Independence was signed July 4th, 1776, *by all present in Congress on that day except Mr. Dickinson*." By this error of judgment he charges his grandfather with the inconsistency of voting against the Declaration in the morning and signing it in the afternoon.

Secretary of the Convention," (as William T. Read himself says in the above work, p. 186,) renders it still more probable that this paper in George Read's handwriting is the identical copy he had before him; since the secretary is the proper one to have supplied the presiding officer with copies of the changes and amendments made from time to time.

A recent visit to Dover disclosed the fact that there are now no manuscript records whatever in the archives of the state, relating to this convention. Even the constitution itself cannot be found. All the records were probably destroyed many years ago. Very likely the records were captured by·the British at the time President McKinly was taken prisoner, as related in a letter of Mr. McKean on a subsequent page.[1] The journals of the convention were, however, published in 1776, by which it appears that the convention met August 27, 1776, George Read being elected president. On the 30th Mr. McKean obtained leave of absence on account of the sickness of his son and sister. He returned September 6th, and the following day with George Read and others was placed on the committee to draft the constitution. The committee reported on the 14th; the matter was read a second time on the 15th, and recommitted; reported again on the 17th. The constitution was partly agreed to on the 18th, and fully approved on the 20th. The convention was dissolved on the 21st.

CHIEF JUSTICE OF PENNSYLVANIA.

On the 28th of July 1777, Mr. McKean received from the Supreme Executive Council, the commission of Chief Justice of Pennsylvania; the duties of which high station he performed with zeal and fidelity for twenty-two years. At the time of his appointment, he was Speaker of the House of Assembly of Delaware, and a delegate in Congress from that State. Six weeks later he became President of Delaware. He took the oath of office September 1st following; and was subsequently reappointed July 29, 1784, and July 29, 1791.[2]

The period during which Mr. McKean exercised the functions of Chief Justice, was one of the most important and trying in the whole course of the jurisprudence of the commonwealth. It was at the time when the laws were unsettled, even the constitutions of the states undefined, and national existence

---

[1] See also Appleton's Cyclop. Biog. McKinly, iv., 137.

[2] Scharf and Westcott, ii., 1559; Hazard's Penn. Archives, v., 621.

itself in question. The country was in the midst of a revolution when he came to the bench; and for several years the civil was necessarily subordinate to the military rule. Hence the interpretation of organic and statute law had to be made *de novo;* precedents had to be established, and the whole practice of the courts adapted to the changed relations which existed. The causes which were brought in his court were many of them peculiar to a period of war and conquest;—causes involving the most delicate questions, vital alike to the rights of the subject, and the vindication of justice. Trials for high treason, for attainder, for the confiscation of property, were frequent. A case rarely transcended in importance and amount involved, in any nation or in any age, was the forfeiture of the proprietary estates. The rulings of the chief justice, through all this trying period, and in their different causes were marked by great prudence and wisdom.[1]

" Chief Jestice McKean," observes a late Judge of the Supreme Court, " was a great man; his merit in the profession of the law and as a judge, has never been sufficiently appreciated. It is only since I have been upon the bench that I have been able to conceive a just idea of the greatness of his merit. His legal learning was profound and accurate ; but in the words of the poet—

> *Materiam superbat opus.—*

The lucidity of his explication, and the perspicuity of his language, which is the first excellence in the communication of ideas, was perfect; but I never saw equalled his dignity of manner in delivering a charge to a jury, or on a law argument to the bar. But what is still more, his comprehension of mind in taking notes, so as to embrace the *substance,* and yet emit nothing *material,* has appeared to be inimitable."[2]

"All subsequent decisions of the Supreme Court have sanctioned his judicial fame, and even European judges yielded to him spontaneous praise."[3]

Having heard the opinions of a judge, let us now turn to those of the advocate: David Paul Brown, who achieved an enviable distinction at the Philadelphia bar,[4] writes that Chief Justice McKean " was always considered a sound lawyer and an upright judge ; . . he was a stern and arbitrary man. . . . Though always deemed a very able lawyer, and a man of in-

[1] Armor, *Lives of the Governors of Penn.*

[2] Ibid., and also as quoted in Sanderson's *Lives.* Author unknown.

[3] *The Supreme Court Bench of Pennsylvania,* in Hazard's Reg., iii., 241, a similar article to the previous, and probably by the same author.

[4] *The Forum,* i., 327, *et seq.*

flexible honesty, was still a man of strong prejudices, jealous
of his authority, and rough and overbearing in its maintainance.
. . . Whatever may have been his deficiency in civility, he
was a judge of great decision and force of character. During
the course of his long judicial life, he never wavered in what
his duty seemed to require."

L. Carroll Judson, also a member of the Philadelphia bar,
says, in his beautifully written biography:[1]

"No threats could intimidate, or influence reach him when
designed to divert him from the independent discharge of his duty.
His profound legal acquirements, his ardent zeal, his great justice,
his vigorous energy, and his noble patriotism enabled him to out-
ride every storm, and calm the raging billows that often surrounded
him. . . . . His legal opinions, based as they generally are, upon the
firm pillar of equal justice, strict equity, and correct law,—given
as they were, when a form of government was changing, the laws
unsettled, our state constitutions justformed, the federal constitution bursting into embryo,—are monuments of fame, enduring
as social order, respected and cononized."

" He was without exception one of the greatest legal minds in
our early history ; filling every station with distinguished zeal and
fidelity,—a man of eminent learning, ability and integrity, whom
neither fear nor favor could bend from the stern line of duty."[2]

With two more quotations I will close these extracts, my
purpose being to show that praise of the legal and judicial
fame of Thomas McKean is not confined to the writings of a
few; but is universally proclaimed by all his biographers.
The following is from another beautifully written biography by
David R. B. Nevin.[3]

"Of McKean as a lawyer, we may safely say he was master of
that intricate profession. As a contemporary remarked of Tilghman, we may appropriately say of McKean, ' he took in at one
glance all the beauties of the most obscure and difficult litigations.
With him it was intuitive, and he could untie the knots of a con-
tingent remainder, or an executive device, as familiarly as he
could his garter.' Of his career as a judge, it is unnecessary for
us to comment; for his judicial fame is the common property of
the world. Pennsylvania, however much she may have suffered
in many instances by irresponsible and unworthy political representatives in the councils of the nation, has always been justly
proud of her incorruptible and learned judiciary. Ross, Tilgh-

[1] *Biography of the Signers*, 1839.
[2] W. II. Egle, in *Penn. Mag.*, xi., 250 ; *The Fed. Const., Sketches, etc.*
[3] *Continental Sketches of Distinguished Pennsylvanians*, 1875.

man, Ingersoll, Rawle, and Bradford, with a host of others, were brilliant stars in the legal firmament of the old colonial times; and the lustre of the galaxy has not been dimmed by such modern luminaries as Gibson and Black. But the peer of them all was Chief Justice McKean. A faultless logician, fluent without the least volubiliiy, wonderfully concise, with a naturally logical mind, well disciplined by severe and systematic training, he was a most brilliant advocate and attorney. As a judge he had few equals in this or any other.land. When he assumed the judicial ermine, the laws of Pennsylvania were crude and unsettled; and it devolved upon him to overcome all these difficulties, and bring order out of comparative chaos. His decisions were remarkably accurate, sometimes quite profound, and always delivered with a grace of diction, and a perspicuity of language, which commended them to the cultivated legal mind. His personal appearance on the bench was a combination of proper affibility and great dignity."

We have heard the words of his friends—it is but just to give ear to one of his opponents,[1] who says of Chief Justice McKean:

"He was well qualified for the office of Chief Justice, by his power to reason, discriminate and combine; his great learning, and ready use of it; his courage, firmness, and inflexibility; but little accessible to pleadings for mercy, and so much the slave of party, (as appears by the authority cited in the sequel to this sketch,) as to lend more than once, his judicial power to punish its enemies and still more his own."[2]

Other extracts may be found in the various biographies of Chief Justice McKean, too numerous to be inserted here.[3]

NOTED CASES.

The cases decided by Chief Justice McKean are contained in Alexander J. Dallas' Reports of Pennsylvania cases, in four volumes, 1754 to 1806. The first volume was published

---

[1] Of those writing since Judge McKean's death, I have found but *two* who have written against him. See note at end of this biography.

[2] *Life of Geo. Read*, by his grandson, William T. Read, 1870, p. 335. The fact that McKean sent an express for Cæsar Rodney and outvoted Read on the Declaration, seems to rankle in the heart of the grandson, who spares no opportunity throughout the whole of his work to speak against Judge McKean. This is to be regretted, as McKean and Read were friends, as well as colleagues and compatriots.

[3] The principle of which may be named: *National Portraits*, by Longacre and Herring, 1839; Hazard's *Reg. of Penn.*, 1829, iii., 241; *Hist. Chester Co., Penn.*, by John Smith Futhey (Judge of the Chester Co. Court) and Gilbert Cope, besides other extracts in the various works already quoted.

in 1790, and the series dedicated to Chief Justice McKean. The other volumes appeared successively in 1798, 1799, and 1807. Lord Mansfield, then in his advanced years, upon receiving the first volume from Judge McKean, in 1791, sent the following in reply: "I am not able to write with my own hand, and most therefore beg leave to make use of another, to acknowledge the honor you have done me by your most obliging and elegant letter, and sending me Dallas' reports. I am not able to read myself, but have heard them all read with much pleasure. They do credit to the court, the bar, and the reporter. They show readiness in practice, liberality in principle, strong reason, and legal learning. The method too is clear and the language pure."[1]

Among the more prominent cases which came before Chief Justice McKean may be mentioned the following:

Roberts and Carlisle (1 Dallas, 35, 39). When the British took possession of Philadelphia, John Roberts enlisted in the British army, and tried to induce others to do the same. Abraham Carlisle was a carpenter, who received a commission from Sir William Howe to watch and guard the gates of the city, with power of granting passports. They were attainted for high treason, and the trial came in September, 1778. Joseph Reed was the leading counsel on the part of the State. The just performance of Chief Justice McKean's judicial functions during this time of war required not only the learning of the lawyer, but the unyielding spirit of the patriot. Proclaiming from the bench the law of justice and his country, with distinguished learning, ability and integrity, neither fear nor power could bend him from the stern line of duty. Regardless of the powers of the crown of Great Britain, he did not hesitate to hazard his own life by causing to be punished, even unto death, those who were proved to be traitors to their country.[2]

The fate of these men caused great excitement generally, and especially among the Quakers, to which sect they belonged. The Supreme Executive Council was deluged with petitions for clemency; private citizens sent a score of petitions, the ministers of the gospel, the grand jury, the jury which tried them; even the judiciary, Chief Justice McKean and Judge Evans, petitioned the Council for a postponement of the execution. Chief Justice McKean's notes of the trial were sent to the

---

[1] MSS. McKean family, Binghamton, and partly quoted in Hazard's *Reg. of Penn.*, iii., 241 *et seq.*

[2] Sanderson's *Lives.* See also Hazard's *Reg.*, iii., 241.

Council for their information.[1] It appears from this that Roberts and Carlisle were the lamented victims of inflexible justice. The petition of the Chief Justice shows that he did not deserve the censure bestowed upon him by the quakers and tories, both in prose and verse; he simply performed his duty in passing sentence, the execution of which rested with the Supreme Executive Council, who could have pardoned the prisoners if they had found sufficient cause to do so.

Samuel Chapman (1 Dallas, 53) was also attainted for high treason in the April term, 1781, for not having surrendered himself on the 1st of August, 1778, as required by a proclamation issued by the Supreme Executive Council, in pursuance of an act of the Assembly passed March 6, 1778. The charge of the Chief Justice, which resulted in the acquittal of the defendant, was learned and circumstantial, embracing a lucid exposition of the law, and exciting the unqualified admiration of his professional brethren; while it dissatisfied and disappointed those men who thirsted after blood. No popular excitement against individuals accused of offences could in the slightest degree divert Chief Justice McKean from the firm and inflexible discharge of his public duty. His decision evinced the soundness of his judgment, and the disdain he felt for the popular clamor excited by the occasion.[2]

A writ of Habeas Corpus. Soon after his appointment as Chief Justice, an incident occurred evincing in bold relief, the independent principle of action which guided his judicial career. Twenty persons were confined in the Free-Mason's lodge at Philadelphia, on treasonable charges; and the popular excitement against them was extremely violent. They published a remonstrance in the Pennsylvania Packet of September 5, 1777; and application was made to the Chief Justice for writs of *habeas corpus* in their behalf, which were granted. This act, at a period of peculiar public agitation, created great dissatisfaction among the more violent whigs, in which many members of Congress participated. So marked was their displeasure, that Judge McKean, esteeming the good opinion of good men, next to the approbation of a good conscience, wrote to John Adams on the subject, explaining his course of action. For a statement of Judge McKean's position in this matter, the reader is referred to Sanderson's Lives; suffice it here to say in brief, that Judge McKean had followed the Pennsylvania

---

[1] *Penn. Archives*, Hazard, 1853, vii., 21, 25, 44, 53, *etc.*
[2] Sanderson's *Lives.*

statute, which had somewhat modified the laws regarding *habeas corpus*, and by which all discretionary power in the judges was taken away, and a penalty of five hundred pounds imposed for a refusal to grant a writ.[1]

The popular excitement against these tories was so great that the Assembly passed a law suspending the writ of *habeas corpus*, thus preventing the execution of Judge McKean's writ. William Allen, a lawyer and a tory, in his *Journal* calls this "a law *ex post facto* and *pendente lite*, the very extreme of tyranny."[2]

Warrant against Colonel Hooper. Judge McKean's firmness in the execution of the law is exemplified by another striking example. In 1778 he issued a warrant against Colonel Robert L. Hooper, deputy quartermaster, charging him with having libelled the magistrates in a letter to Gouverneur Morris; and directing the sheriff of Northampton county to bring the said Hooper before him at Yorktown. Colonel Hooper waited on General Green, who wrote to Judge Mc-Kean that he could not consent to Colonel Hooper's absence. To this letter, the reply of the Chief Justice, under date of June 9, 1778, contains the following characteristic paragraph:

"I do not think, sir, that the absence, sickness, or even death of Mr. Hooper could be attended with such consequences that *no other person* could be found, who could give the necessary aid upon this occasion; but, what attracts my attention the most, is your observation that *you* cannot, without great necessity, *consent to his being absent.* As to that, sir, I shall not ask *your consent,* nor that of any other person, in or out of the army, whether my precept shall be obeyed or not in Pennsylvania."

There is a strain of inflexible firmness and unshrinking dignity pervading this letter, admirably illustrative of the whole course of his judicial conduct.[3]

The House of Assembly having asked the opinion of Chief Justice McKean as to the right of the crown to grant the charter to the Penns: he gave his opinion upon the question, which was afterwards judicially determined in the case of Penn's lessee *vs.* Kline, before Justice Washington of the Supreme Court of the United States, and Richard Peters, District Judge (4 Dallas, 402).[4]

---

[1] Sanderson's *Lives.*

[2] Under date of Oct. 1, 1777, published in *Pa. Mag.,* ix., 293.

[3] Sanderson's *Lives.*

[4] *Life of Joseph Reed,* William B. Reed, 1847, ii., 167.

In the *Issues of the Press* of Pennsylvania, by Charles R. Hildeburn, 1886, there is noted No. 3738, the following work, " Charge of Thomas McKean, Chief Justice, to Grand Jury at Court of Oyer and Terminer and General Gaol Delivery held at York," 1788.

INCIDENTS AND ANECDOTES.

It is related of Chief Justice McKean, by a contemporary, that ",the Chief Justice when on the bench wore an immense cocked-hat, and was dressed in a scarlet gown. He discharged the office of chief justice for twenty-two years, and gave striking proofs of ability, impartiality and courage."[1]

Watson, the antiquarian, in his chapter on wigs, relates that " Judge McKean wore one, and was withal so partial to them that he intended to wear one of the bench kind; he engaged one of Kyd for one hundred dollars, and being found when de livered, so strange and *outré* he refused it, and was sued for the value."[2]

In those days it was the custom of the Supreme Court to hold sessions in the various counties. When at Harrisburg— at least while Congress sat at York—(1777-8), Chief Justice McKean lived in a substantial one-story log house, a short space below what is now Locust street. He wore an immense cocked-hat, and had great deference shown him by the country people. After the country was quieted, when he and other judges of the Supreme Court came to Harrisburg to hold court, numbers of the citizens of the place would go out on horseback to meet them, and escort them to town. Sometimes one or two hundred people would attend for the purpose. The sheriff with his rod of office, and other public officers and bar, would attend on the occasion; and each morning, while the Chief Justice was in town holding court, the sheriff and constables escorted him from his lodgings to the court-room. The Chief Justice on the bench sat with his hat on, and was dressed in a scarlet gown.[3]

Many anecdotes says David Paul Brown, remain of the great jurist both as Chief Justice and Governor.

One day when a mob had assembled outside of the Supreme

---

[1] *Graydon's Memoirs of His Own Time*, 1846. See also *Manasseh Cutler's* Journal, 1787; *Pa. Mag.*, xi., 108.

[2] *Annals of Phil.*, 1868, i., 197.

[3] Day's *Histor. Collections*, 1843, p. 286.

5

Court, he sent for the sheriff and commanded him to suppress the riot.

"I cannot do it," replied the trembling official.

"Why do you not summon your *posse*?" thundered the scowling Chief Justice.

"I have summoned them, but they are ineffectual."

"Then sir, why do you not summon *me*?"

The sheriff stunned for a moment, gasped out, "I do summon you, sir."

Whereupon the gigantic Chief Justice, scarlet gown, cocked hat and all, swooped down on the mob like an eagle on a flock of sheep, and catching two of the ringleaders by the throat, quelled the riot.[1]

The talented but unfortunate Major André, at an entertainment at Mr. Deane's in New York, read a characteristic *Dream;* "His allusions," says a loyalist commentator, "to Jackey Jay, Paddy McKean, and other rebellious —— were excellent."

André dreamed he was in a spacious apartment in which the infernal judges were dispensing justice.

"As dreams are of an unaccountable nature" he says, "it will not (I presume,) be thought strange that I should behold upon this occasion the shades of many who for aught I know may be still living. . . . The first person called upon was the famous Chief Justice McKean, who I found had been animated by the same spirit which formerly possessed the memorable Jeffreys. I could not but observe a flush of indignation in the eyes of the judges upon the approach of this culprit. His more than savage cruelty, his horrid disregard to the many oaths of allegiance he had taken, and the vile sacrifices he had made of justice, to the interests of rebellion, were openly rehearsed. Notwithstanding his common impudence, for once, he seemed abashed, and did not pretend to deny the charge. He was condemned to assume the shape of a blood-hound, and the souls of Roberts and Carlisle were ordered to scourge him through the infernal regions." Next appeared the "polite and traveled Mr. Deane:" then "the celebrated General Lee;" "the black soul of Livingston:" "The President of Congress, Mr. Jay," and finally "the whole continental army," each of whom was "judged" in some characteristic manner.[2]

Another loyalist, now unknown, has left a long poem from which the following extracts are made:

---

[1] *The Forum*, as quoted by Rebecca Harding Davis in *Harper's Mag.*, 1876, lii., 871.

[2] Frank Moore's *Diary of Am. Rev.*, N. Y., 1860, ii., 120 *et seq.*

THE AMERICAN TIMES; A SATIRE, BY CAMILLO QUERNO.

Hear thy indictment, Washington, at large;
Attend and listen to the solemn charge:
*   *   *   *   *   *   *   *
Wilt thou pretend that Britain is in fault?
In Reason's court a falsehood goes for nought.
Will it avail, with subterfuge refin'd
To say such deeds are foreign to thy mind?
Wilt thou assert that, generous and humane,
Thy nature suffers at another's pain?
He who a band of ruffians keeps to kill,
Is he not guilty of the blood they spill?
Who guards McKean and Joseph Reed the vile,
Help'd he not to murder Roberts and Carlisle?
So, who protects committees in the chair,
In all their shocking cruelties must share.
*   *   .*   *   *   *   *   *
Bring up your wretched solitary pair,
Mark'd with pride, malice, envy, rage, despair,
Why are you banish'd from your comrades, tell?
Will none endure your company in hell?
That all the fiends avoid your sight is plain,
Infamous Reed, more infamous McKean.
Is this the order of your rank agreed;
Or is it base McKean and baser Reed?
Go, shunn'd of men, disown'd of devils, go,
And traverse desolate the realms of woe.[1]

PRESIDENT OF THE STATE OF DELAWARE.

In September 1777, Judge McKean became the executive of the state of Delaware. It is stated in the *Life of George Read*,[2] that the presidency of Delaware was offered to Mr. Read who declined it, and Mr. McKinly was appointed. When the latter gentleman was captured by the British, Judge McKean immediately assumed the reins of government.

Under date of October 8, 1777, Judge McKean writes to General Washington from Newark, "By the captivity of President McKinly of the Delaware State, on the 12th of last month, and the absence of the Vice-President, the command in chief devolved upon me as Speaker of the Assembly, agreeably to the constitution. I had some time before accepted the office of Chief Justice of Pennsylvania, and at the time this

---

[1] *Loyalist Poetry of the Rev.*, Winthrop Sargent, Phil., 1857, pp. 10, 11.
[2] By his grandson, William T. Read, 1870.

unfortunate event happened, was out of the Delaware State, but thought it my duty to my country to repair thither, which I did on the 20th following." On his arrival in the state, Judge McKean found that all the papers, public records, and money had been captured. He immediately called out the militia, one-half in active service, and the remainder to hold themselves in readiness for instant service.[1]

When this high position devolved upon Judge McKean, while holding other high offices in Pennsylvania, he became thereby an especial object of British persecution. " I have had," he says in a letter two years afterwards to Mr. Adams, dated November 8, 1779, " I have had my full share of the anxieties, care and troubles of the present war. For some time I was obliged to act as President of the Delaware State, and as Chief Justice of this: general Howe had just landed (August, 1777) at the head of Elk River, when I undertook to discharge these two important trusts. The consequence was, to be hunted like a fox by the enemy, and envied by those who ought to have been my friends. I was compelled to remove my family five times in a few months, and at last fixed them in a little log-house on the banks of the Susquehannah, more than a hundred miles from this place ; but safety was not to be found there ; for they were obliged to remove again on account of the incursions of the Indians."[2]

Judge McKean held this office but a short time, and after making provisions for the defense of the State, addressed a letter to George Read, the Vice-President, under date of September 26, 1777, informs him of his accession to the office, the reasons for it, details his official acts and resigns the position, concluding his letter as follows : " Wishing you all manner of success in saving our country in general, and the Delaware - State in particular, I am," etc. Addressed, " To George Read, President of the Delaware State."[3]

THE ARTICLES OF CONFEDERATION.

The commmitee appointed in Congress, June 12, 1776, pursuant to a resolution of the 7th, to frame the Articles of Confederation, consisted of thirteen members, one for each State, as follows : Josiah Bartlett, Samuel Adams, Stephen Hopkins,

---

[1] Spark's *Corresp. of Rev.*, Boston, 1853, i., 443.
[2] Sanderson.
[3] *Life and Corresp. of Geo. Read.*

Roger Sherman, Robert R. Livingston, John Dickinson, Thomas McKean, Thomas Stone, Thomas Nelson, Jr., Joseph Hewes, Edward Rutledge and Button Gwinnett; on the 28th Francis · Hopkinson was added, completing the number.[1] The Articles were under consideration for several months, and debated clause by clause. On a vote relating to taxation occurred the first important division between the slave hold-·ing states and the states where slavery was of little account.[2] The articles were finally agreed to, November 13, 1777, and a copy being made out the same was agreed to on the 15th. This state paper, which is the first constitution of our country, was dated and signed July 9, 1778, by the delegates of nine states; the other delegates had not then been empowered to sign it. Thomas McKean signed subsequently in behalf of Delaware, pursuant to powers vested in him dated February 6, 1779, and laid before Congress on the 16th.[3] The last State Maryland signed March 1, 1781. This important document is preserved in the archives of the Department of State. It is on parchment in one sheet, a roll about thirteen feet long.

A HISTORICAL DISCREPANCY.

As the other four states ratified the Articles, the delegates added the date of signing. And here, as to the date when Thomas McKean affixed his signature, there is a decided discrepancy between the Journals of Congress and the original Articles of Confederation, which seems to have escaped the notice of historians. In the Journals of Congress, (the original rough Journal by Charles Thomson, which I have had the privilege of examining, page 265,) is the entry, February 22, 1779. "In pursuance of the powers in him vested, Mr. McKean a delegate of the state of Delaware, signed and ratified the articles of Confederation in behalf of that state." (See the Printed Journals, Way and Gideon, 1823, iii., 201.) In the original Articles, the date is now much obliterated, but is apparently "Feb. 12, 1779;" the word "*Feb.*" is almost illegible, the first figure apparently 1 is a heavy stroke with a dot after it, the lower part of the 2 is wholly illegible and also has a dot following it. There is no trace remaining, even

---

[1] *Journals of Congress;* Adams' *Works,* ii., 292; Frothingham, p. 569. The following authors give but *twelve* names: *Hist. Old State House.* Etting; Lossing's *Field Book,* 1860, ii., 653; Scharf and Westcott, *Hist. Phil.,* i., 315.

[2] Bancroft's *U. S.*

[3] *Journals of Congress,* Feb. 16–22, 1879.

under a glass to show that the first figure was a 2 obliterated. Upon the articles being ratified by all the states, they are entered upon the Journal under date of March 1, 1781, where the date is given " Feb. 12, 1779." (1st ed., Patterson, vii. 48, and Way and Gideon 1823, iii., 591). In the Secret Journal, however, (Thomas B. Wait, 1821, i. 448–64,) a por-
. tion of the volume is devoted to debates on the Articles. They are entered at length, upon the Journal and the date given in full " February 22, 1779," agreeing with the first date in the rough Journal. But there is also a discrepancy between the Rough and Secret Journal, under date of March 1, 1781.

Hoping to clear up the discrepancy by an examination of early published copies, I found to my surprise, that in older publications the date is usually given neither 12th nor 22d, but " Feb. 18, 1779," and so given in the *Laws of the U. S.*, [John B. Calvin,] 1815; *The Federalist*, New ed. 1837, p. 480 ; and *Elliot's Debates*, 1854, i. 85.

In other publications and later works the date is given February 12, 1779, viz.: *U. S. Statutes at Large*, Richard Peters, 1845; *Hickey's Constitution*, 1855, p. 490; *Fed. and State Const.*, B. P. Poore, 1877 ; *Documents Illust. Amer. Hist.*, Preston, 1886.

Other works too numerous to mention, some of them pub-lished during the last century, give the Articles and names, but omit the dates. Others omit the names also. *McKean's Laws*, 1782, and Dallas' *Laws of Pennsylvania*, 1797, might have settled the discrepancy, especially the former work, but they give the names without dates.

It is doubtful if the discrepancy can ever be cleared up; February 22, 1779, seems, however, to be the most reliable date, for that entry in the journal was undoubtedly made on - that date ; and as Mr. McKean's authority to sign was laid be-fore Congress on the 16th, and entered in the journal on that day, it does not seem likely that he would sign before the lat-ter date. Lossing, in his " Lives of the Signers," appends an account of the Articles of Confederation, and states that Dela-ware ratified " on the twenty-second of February and 5th of May, 1779."[1]

About this time, Thomas McKean took the oath of allegiance before his relative and former preceptor, David Finney, dated January 25, 1779, that he does not hold himself bound to yield any allegiance to the king of Great Britain, but will be true

---

[1] Ed. 1860, p. 327.

and faithful to the Delaware State.[1] Various judges, public officers, members of Congress and others took the oath about this same time.

DIFFICULTY WITH GENERAL THOMPSON.

This officer had been a prisoner of war, and when released on parole became angry because he had not been exchanged; and said that Congress had treated him in a " rascally manner." He was particularly bitter against Judge McKean, whom he accused of having hindered his exchange; and denounced him for having acted " like a liar, a rascal, and a coward." Judge McKean laid the matter before Congress, November 19, 1778, in an information of personal abuse; whereupon General Thompson was called before the bar of the house, and apologized.[2]

The Supreme Executive Council, December 31, 1778, also took notice of the " acrimonious remarks by Brigadier General William Thompson."[3] Judge McKean moreover sued Thompson, and got judgment for the large sum of £5,700 against him and the publishers of the *Packet*. McKean, however, released the damages in both cases, as he only wanted to see the law and the facts settled. Thompson then tried to provoke a duel with McKean; but McKean would not set the precedent of allowing a member of Congress or a magistrate to subject himself to a duel with every person against whom he gave judgment.[4]

MEETING OF MAY 24–25, 1779.

This public meeting was called to counteract the effect of monopolizers, and to devise means to reduce prices. General Daniel Roberdeau, recently a delegate in Congress, and a signer of the Articles of Confederation, was called to the chair; Timothy Matlack, David Rittenhouse, Thomas Paine, Charles W. Peale, Thomas McKean, and others, were present. A committee, appointed to carry out the purposes of the meeting, was made permanent. " The institution of this committee," it is remarked in the *Life of Joseph Reed*, " is a leading incident in the local history of these times." The meeting also resolved that " those inimical to independence should not be

---

[1] Original in possession of J. Henry Rogers, Esq.

[2] *Journals of Cong.*, Nov. 19–23, 1778.

[3] Hazard's *Colonial Records*, xi., 653.

[4] Scharf and Westcott, *Hist. Phil.*, i., 393.

suffered to remain among us." An account of the meeting is given in full in the *Genealogy of the Roberdeau Family.*[1] A pamphlet in regard to this meeting, entitled " Meeting of May 25, 1779," was published by Daniel Roberdeau, the chairman.[2]

The tories, who let no opportunity pass for ridiculing the public characters of the day, published a poem, of which the following is a portion:

AN HISTORICAL BALLAD OF THE PROCEEDINGS OF A TOWN MEETING AT PHILADELPHIA, MAY 24-5, 1779.—BY STANSBERRY.

'Twas on the twenty-fourth of May,
A pleasant, warm, sunshiny day,
    Militia folks paraded,
With colors spread, and cannon too,
Such loud huzzas, and martial view,
    I thought the town invaded.

And now the State-House yard was full,
And orators, so grave and, dull,
    Appear'd upon the stage,
But all was riot, noise, disgrace,
And freedom's sons, o'er all the place,
    In bloody frays engage.

Each vagrant from the whipping-post,
Or stranger stranded on the coast,
    May here reform the State,
And Peter, Mick, and Shad-row Jack,
And Pompey-like McKean in black,
    Decide a people's fate.
   *   *   *   *   *

With solemn phiz and action slow,
Arose the chairman *Roberdeau,*
    And made the humane motion,
That tories, with their brats and wives,
Should flee to save their wretched lives,
    From Sodom to Goshen.[3]

HIGH COURT OF ERRORS AND APPEALS.

To this court, which was established by the Act of February 28, 1780, Judge McKean was commissioned with seven others,

---

[1] See also *Penn. Packet,* May 27, 1779 ; *Life of Joseph Reed,* W. B. Reed.
[2] Catalogued in Hildeburn's *Issues of Press of Penn.,* 1886, No. 3951.
[3] Watson's *Annals of Phil.*

November 20, 1780. The court was reorganized under the Act of April 13, 1791, and he was recommissioned with nine others, April 13, 1791. The court was abolished by Act of February 24, 1806. Judge McKean retained his seat as Chief Justice during this time.[1]

During this year, 1780, there was an urgent need of funds, and a few patriotic gentlemen subscribed $260,000; the Bank of Pennsylvania was then organized for the purpose of supplying the army with provisions; for this purpose Judge McKean subscribed £2000.[2]

On the 25th of December of this same year Judge McKean, in a letter to the legislature of Delaware, resigned his seat in Congress. "I find," said he, "that my health and fortune are impaired by my unremitted attention to public affairs; what I undertake to perform, I do with all my might; and having very little relief in attending Congress, I find that this, the discharging the duties of Chief Justice, etc., etc., are more than I can perform to my own satisfaction. Besides, the rank I am obliged to maintain is greater than comports with my finances." . . . It is a proof of the disinterested principles by which the public men of that period were guided, that Mr. McKean had never received, in any year, as much emolument, as a delegate, as would defray his personal expenses while engaged in the service; and that during the last two years, (1779 and 1780,) he had not been offered or received a farthing. His resignation, however, was not accepted, and he continued his duties as a delegate from Delaware.[3]

HIS RESIDENCE.

Chief Justice McKean's residence being mentioned by various writers, a description should not be omitted here. For some years, according to Lossing, he resided in High street, now known as Market street, near Second. But in 1780, December 20th, the Supreme Executive Council directed that the honorable Chief Justice McKean be allowed to occupy Mr. Duché's house until July 1st next. In explanation of this, it may be stated that the Rev. Mr. Duché had been chaplain to the first continental Congress; but being of a vacillating character, after siding with the colonists, joined the British and went to

---

[1] Scharf and Westcott, ii., 1568 ; *Bench and Bar of Phil.*, John Hill Martin.

[2] Scharf and Westcott, i., 409 ; Niles' *Principles and Acts of the Rev.*

[3] Sanderson.

England.[1] He was attainted for high treason, and his property confiscated. This property consisting of the mansion,
coach house, stables and four lots, was sold August 10, 1781,
to Thomas McKean for £7750, Pennsylvania currency, subject
to a ground rent of 232½ bushels of wheat. A deed for the
property bearing the above date was executed by the Supreme
Executive Council, in which the property is described as being
on the east side of Third street, occupying the whole side
of the square from Pine street on the south to Union street
on the north, and thirty feet in depth.[2] This building is described in the *Historic Mansions and Buildings of Philadelphia*[3] as " a large and splendid mansion in the Elizabethan
style at the northeast corner of Third and Pine streets." An
engraving of the house is given in various works;—in the *Book
of the Signers*, by William Brotherhead, 1861, folio; in
Sanderson's *Biography of the Signers*, revised by R. T.
Conrad, 4°; in Watson's *Annals of Philadelphia*, (3 vols.
revised by Willis P. Hazard, 1884, i., 413;) and in Scharf and
Westcott's *History of Philadelphia*, i., 292. There was a
large hall in this house, at the ends of which hung the two
portraits by Peale, of Chief Justice McKean with his son
standing by his side, and of his wife Sarah Armitage with a
child on her lap. The mansion passed by will to the eldest
son, Judge Joseph B. McKean.

PRESIDENT OF CONGRESS.

To this exalted position, the highest in the gift of the people
or of Congress, Judge McKean was elected on the resignation
of Samuel Huntington, on the 10th of July, 1781. General
Washington sent his congratulations to him under date of July
21.[4] Being also Chief Justice of Pennsylvania, his holding
two such high positions at one time raised a clamor of opposition to him. The press teemed with essays upon the subject,
maintaining both sides of the question; in which the advocates
of Mr. McKean enjoyed a manifest advantage. The chief
point alleged was, that it was illegal to hold the office of Chief
Justice while sitting in Congress; but it is evident that the
authors of the outcry were incited either by envy or ambition,
and not by virtue or love of country, because if his seat was

[1] See his life in Keith's *Provinc. Councillors*, p. 276.
[2] *Penn. Colo. Records*, xii., 578, xiii., 25 ; Scharf and Westcott, i. 420.
[3] Thompson Westcott, 1877, p. 90.
[4] *Writings of Washington*, Jared Sparks, 12 vols., Boston, 1837, viii., 112.

illegal at all, it was as much so before he was made president as afterwards. The Constitution of Pennsylvania, indeed, forbade the holding of two offices; but it was contended that this did not apply to holding other offices outside of the State; so that his being a member of Congress from Delaware would not conflict with the Constitution of Pennsylvania when he became Chief Justice. The outcry came chiefly from Pennsylvania, which was unreasonable considering that Pennsylvania had appointed the Delaware member of Congress as Chief Justice. It was moreover shown that several others were then holding these two offices in various States. It was decided that he could hold both offices; the foundation of the decision was, that one State could not interfere with another in its internal administration, which included the selection of its officers. Delaware could not interfere with the selection of the Pennsylvania Chief Justice, nor could Pennsylvania restrain Delaware in her selection of members of Congress; and Judge McKean's seat was properly held and his election as President was valid.[1]

On Sunday, September 2d of this year, the American army passed through to Philadelphia going south; followed on the 3d and 4th by the French troops. As the latter passed through, they were reviewed by Thomas McKean, President of Congress, who on this occasion, appeared in black velvet with a sword at his side, and his head covered. On his left were Washington and Rochambeau uncovered; and on his right M. de Luzerne, the French minister. As the officers saluted in passing, McKean responded by removing his hat; and afterwards complimented the appearance of the various corps.[2]

These were the troops marching to victory at Yorktown, and not many weeks afterwards, Colonel Tilghman, one of Washington's *aides-de-camp* rode express to Philadelphia, to carry the dispatches of his chief, announcing to Congress the joyful tidings of the surrender of Cornwallis. "It was midnight when he entered the city, October 23, 1781. Thomas McKean the President of Congress resided in High street,[3] near Second. Tilghman knocked at the door so vehemently that a watchman was disposed to arrest him for disturbing the

---

[1] Sanderson's *Lives.*

[2] Scharf and Westcott, i., 415. Also Thacher's *Military Journal,* Boston, 1827.

[3] Probably a mistake, as he had recently removed to Third stree

72   MCKEAN FAMILY.

peace. McKean arose, and presently the glad tidings were
made known."[1] And as the watchman—an old German
named Hurry—called the hour he proclaimed in a loud sonor-
ous voice, " *Basht dree o'clock and Gornwallis isht daken.*[2]
The dispatches were read to Congress at an early hour the
next morning; and Congress, the same day went in procession
to the Dutch Lutheran Church, to return thanks to Almighty
God for the successes of the allied armies of the United States
and France. Handbills were printed, dated October 24, 1781,
announcing in large letters : ILLUMINATION,—that Colonel
Tilghman having brought news of the surrender, citizens will
illuminate this evening from 6 to 9 oclock.[3]

As the time approached for the Supreme Court to meet,
Mr. McKean, on the 23d of October, 1781, addressed a letter
to Congress resigning the presidency. Congress accepted the
resignation on that day ; but postponed the election of a president until the next day, when on motion of Mr. Witherspoon,
it was unanimously resolved that Mr. McKean be requested to
resume the chair, and act as president, until the 1st Monday in
November. To this he acceded ; and on the 5th, John
Hanson was elected president. On the 7th a vote of thanks
was given to Mr. McKean for his services as president.

THREE REMARKABLE INCIDENTS.

Three remarkable incidents in the life of Thomas McKean
deserve especial mention. The first is, that he is the only
member of the continental congress who retained his seat
successively, with the exception of one year, from the Stamp
Act Congress in 1765, and the first continental congress in
1774, to the peace in 1783. Pennsylvania members were
limited by her constitution to a term of two years ; but Dela- ‾
ware did not so limit her delegates.

The second incident is, that while sitting in congress as a
delegate from Delaware, he was appointed Chief Justice of
Pennsylvania ;—both states claiming him, and holding high
offices in each.

---

[1] Lossing's *Field Book of Rev.*, 1852, ii., 527.

[2] Scharf and Westcott, i., 415–16. This work states that the first news
was received by a messenger at 3 a. m., October 22, and that Col. Tilghman
arrived on the 24th, confirming the news; whereupon the event was celebrated.

[3] Original in possession of Henry Pettit, Esq. A *fac-simile* is given in J. J.
Smith's *Amer. Hist. and Lit. Curiosities*, N. Y., 1860, pl. lx.

The third is the number of high offices he held at one and the same time. While sitting as a delegate from Delaware in Congress, and the chief justice of Pennsylvania, he was a member of the Delaware Assembly and also Speaker, and for a while became *ex officio* President of the State of Delaware and commander in chief. The year before this, he was a colonel of the Pennsylvania Associators, and Chairman of the Committee of Inspection and Observation. Subsequently he held at the same time, the three offices of delegate from Delaware, Chief Justice of Pennsylvania, and President of Congress. In later years he was Governor of Pennsylvania as will be seen further on.

When we reflect upon the number of offices he held, we can form an estimate of the vast labor he performed, and the unwearied application requisite to master the complicated details of litigated cases, essential to the faithful performance of his judicial duties. Yet amidst the violence of party animosity, in which he was extensively involved, although his holding so many offices became the grounds of complaint, yet his enemies do not seem to have charged him with any neglect of his duties.[1]

PUBLISHES THE LAWS OF PENNSYLVANIA.

As already noted in a quotation from a letter of Judge McKean, he was appointed by the Legislature in 1781 to compile the laws of Pennsylvania; which were published the next year with the following title:

" The Acts of the General Assembly of the Commonwealth of Pennsylvania, carefully compared with the originals; and an Appendix containing the laws now in force, passed between the 30th day of September 1775 and the Revolution; together with the Declaration of Independence, the Constitution of the State of Pennsylvania, and the Articles of Confederation of the United States of America. Published by order of the General Assembly, [Arms of the State] Philadelphia, Printed and sold by Francis Bailey in Market street. MDCCLXXXII."

On the next page is given the resolution of the Assembly April 2, 1781, that Thomas McKean should publish the laws; And below this is his certificate that he has caused this volume to be published. The work is briefly known as *McKean's Laws*.[2]

---

[1] *National Portraits*, J. B. Longacre and James Herring, vol. for 1839.

[2] See John Hill Martin's *Bench and Bar of Phil.*, 1883, pp. 185–8; and Hildeburn's *Issues of the Press of Pa.*, 1886, ii., 382, No. 4179.

CONVENTION TO RATIFY THE CONSTITUTION OF THE UNITED
STATES.

About three years after the treaty of peace was signed, a
convention was called to meet in Philadelphia, May 14, 1787,
to frame a constitution for the United States. General Washington[1] presided, and after a session of four months the convention adjourned September 17th, having agreed to the Constitution.

Judge McKean was not a member of this convention, yet he
was neither inattentive, nor inactive with regard to its proceedings. He had always been an advocate of the just rights of the
smaller, against the overbearing influence and power of the
larger states.[2] A vote by states was insisted upon by him, in
the first congress of 1765, and in that held in Philadelphia in
1774, and the concession was made by the other states. At
the meeting of the federal convention, he delivered to the delegates from Delaware, notes of the arguments used on those occasions, and at the same time offered, in private, his reasons in
support of the security of the smaller states, to members who
represented the larger. His influence prevailed; and the
result was the compromise which pervades the present system.[3]

The constitution having been presented to congress by the
convention, was referred to the several states for ratification.
Pennsylvania after a hotly contested election chose delegates
for that purpose who met in Philadelphia, November 20th,
1787.[4] Judge McKean was a member from Philadelphia.
No business was transacted on the first day. On the 21st the
names were read and a ballot taken for president, which resulted: Muhlenberg 30, McKean 29, Gerry 1. It being
questioned whether any one had a majority, the convention
decided that Mr. Muhlenberg should take the chair.

The history of this convention forms the subject of a recent
work: *Pennsylvania and the Federal Constitution* by John
Bach McMaster, and Frederick D. Stone, published by the
Pennsylvania Historical Society 1888; in which the proceed-

---

[1] He kept a journal of his social movements, which has been published in
the *Penn. Mag.*, xi., 296; and the Philadelphia *Times*, July 31, 1887, etc., in
which he records among other things: "Aug. 18. Dined at Chief Justice
McKean's, and spent the evening at home."

[2] See *Papers of James Madison*, Henry D. Gilpin, 1841, ii., 751–2.

[3] Sanderson's *Lives*. (In the Senate each State has an equal vote, and in
the House a vote according to population.)

[4] Scharf and Westcott's *Phila.*, i., 426, which gives the date wrongly 21st.

ings are detailed at length, and the exciting contests between the two parties narrated. A likeness of Thomas McKean is also given, with a sketch of his life.

The Federalists chose for their leaders Wilson and McKean, who took the management of the proceedings. After certain motions relating to the organization and meetings of the convention, Judge McKean on the 23d, moved that the constitution be read, which was done. On Saturday the 24th he moved that it be read a second time ; and in a short speech said that they were situated in a new position, with no rules or precedents to guide them, and in order to bring the matter before them, he would offer a resolution ; not that he expected it would be decided to-day, or in a week ; and that all those should be heard who were opposed to the constitution. He therefore moved :[1]

"That this Convention do *assent to*, and *ratify*, the Constitution agreed to on the seventeenth of September last, by the Convention of the United States of America, held at Philadelphia."

This motion was seconded by Mr. John Allison. The business was now before the convention ; Mr. Wilson rose and spoke in favor of the motion, in a speech lasting several days. The principal speeches are given in Elliot's *Debates on the Federal Constitution*, four vols., Authorized by Congress, 1836 ; but unfortunately all of them are not reported. The opposition was assailed by legal arguments, by sarcasm, and by ridicule. Judge McKean said in the course of his remarks, that the apprehensions of the opposition respecting the new constitution amounted to this, that *if the sky falls we shall catch larks; if the rivers run dry, we shall catch eels;* and he compared their arguments to a sound, but then it was a mere sound, like *the working of small beer.*[2]

On the 10th, Judge McKean announced that on the 12th he would press for a vote. The debates were closed by a long and eloquent speech by Judge McKean on the 11th, embracing a clear and comprehensive view of the whole subject. He unfolded, in a masterly manner, the principles of free government ; demonstrated the superior advantages of the federal constitution ; and satisfactorily answered every objection which had been suggested. Arranging these objections under ten heads, he

---

[1] Not on Monday, 26th, as given in *Elliott's Debates*. This error is pointed out by Bancroft, *United States*, 1885, vi., 384 ; and *Hist. Formation Const. U. S.*, 1885, p. 384.

[2] *Penna. and the Fed. Const.*, 365.

considered them singly, and delivered his refutation of them
in a lucid and forcible manner.   He concluded this powerful
argument in these words :

" The objections to this constitution having been answered, and
all done away, it remains pure and unhurt ; and this alone as' a
forcible argument of its goodness.   *   *   *   The law, sir, has
been my study from my infancy, and my only profession.   I have
gone through the circle of offices, in the legislative, executive and
judicial departments of government ; and from all my study, observation and experience, I must declare that from a full examination and due consideration of this system, it appears to me *the
best the world has yet seen.*"[1]

The convention was criticised by outsiders in the public press,
and Judge McKean did not fail to receive his share of criticism
and abuse from the opposition.   In more than one part of the
State the excitement developed into a riot.   In Carlisle, in particular, two figures labeled *Thomas McKean Chief Justice,*
and *James Wilson the Caledonian,* were burned by the mob.[2]

Nevertheless a majority of the people approved the constitution ; and the next year a majority of States having ratified
it by the close of June, a procession to celebrate the event was
arranged in Philadelphia for July 4, 1788.   A description of
this celebration from the pen of Francis Hopkinson, chairman
of the committee of arrangements, has been preserved and recently published.

The First City Troop headed the escort: *Independence* was
represented by Colonel John Nixon, who had read the Declaration twelve years before at the State House ; *The French
Alliance,* by Thomas Fitzsimmons ; *The New Æra,* by Richard Bache ; *The Convention of States,* by the Hon. Peter
Muhlenberg on horseback ; THE CONSTITUTION, the Hon.
Chief Justice McKean, the Hon. Judge Atlee, and the Hon.
Judge Rush, in their robes of office, seated in a lofty ornamen-
tal car in the form of an eagle, drawn by six white horses.
The Chief Justice supported a tall staff, on the top of which was
the cap of liberty ; under the cap the NEW CONSTITUTION,
framed and ornamented, and immediately under the constitution the words THE PEOPLE in large gold letters affixed to the
staff.   Next came ten gentlemen of social distinction, representing the ten States which had ratified the constitution ; The

---

[1] Sanderson's *Lives,* and *Elliot's Debates,* 1888, ii., 542.

[2] *Independent Gazetteer,* Jan. 9, 1788, as quoted in *Penn. and Fed. Const.*
p. 488 ; see also McMaster's *Hist. People of U. S.,* i., 475.

Foreign Consuls ; The Hon. Francis Hopkinson, representing the Admiralty ; The Society of the Cincinnati ; various other societies, professions and trades brought up the rear.[1]

THE CASE OF OSWALD, AND IMPEACHMENT PROCEEDINGS.

This case came before the Supreme Court in the July term, 1788.[2] Eleazer Oswald, editor of the *Independent Gazetteer*, was defendant in a suit then pending, and published an article against Andrew Brown. Brown demanded the name of the author, which Oswald declined to give ; he then brought suit, whereupon Oswald on the 10th of July published another piece over his own signature, which was the ground of the case coming before the Supreme Court. Chief Justice McKean considered that the publication would inflame the public, and prejudice those who may be summoned as jurors. He then asked Oswald certain interrogatories, which Oswald refused to answer. Oswald was then, by the unanimous opinion of the judges, held in contempt, and sentenced to a fine of £10, and to be imprisoned " for the space of one month, that is from the 15th day of July to the 15th day of August." The sentence was, however, entered on the record, " for the space of one month," omitting the explanatory words following. At the expiration of the legal month (twenty-eight days), Mr. Oswald demanded his discharge, but this, the sheriff, who had heard the sentence pronounced, refused to grant until he had consulted the Chief Justice. Judge McKean, remembering the meaning and words of the court, told the officer that he was bound to detain his prisoner until the morning of the 15th ; but having shortly afterwards examined the record, he wrote to the sheriff that agreeably to the record there, Mr. Oswald was entitled to his discharge.

On the 5th of September 1788, Mr. Oswald presented a memorial to the General Assembly, in which he stated the proceedings against him, and complained of the decision of the court ; and the direction of the Chief Justice to the sheriff, by which he alleged his confinement had been illegally protracted ; and concluded by asking the impeachment of the judges. The House in committee of the whole, considered this matter three days and examined witnesses. William Lewis made an elaborate argument in vindication of the judges ; Mr. Findley

---

[1] Scharf and Westcott, i., 447 *et seq.;* Philadelphia *Times*, Sept. 11, 1887.
[2] 1 Dallas, 319 ; Scharf and Westcott, i., 426.

6

spoke on the other side, and Mr. Fitzsimmons then made a
motion that there was no cause for impeachment. After
several unimportant motions, one by Mr. Findley claimed the
attention of the house : That the action of the judges was an
unconstitutional exercise of power; and directing the next
Assembly to define the nature and extent of contempts and
direct their punishment. Mr. Findley ably supported his
resolution ; but Mr. Lewis[1] satisfactorily answered him, that
the legislative power is confined to *making* the law, and cannot interfere in the *interpretation*, which is the natural and
exclusive province of the judiciary ; and secondly, the recommendation to the succeeding assembly would be nugatory, for
the courts of justice derive their powers from the constitution,
a source paramount to the legislature, and consequently what
is given to them by the former cannot be taken away by the
latter. Mr. Findley's motion was lost by a considerable majority, and Mr. Clymer then renewed Mr. Fitzsimmons' original
motion, which was adopted, and the memorial of course rejected.[2]

In pronouncing the judgment of the court in the case of Oswald, Chief Justice McKean made the following remarks :

" Some doubts were suggested whether even a contempt of the
court was punishable by attachment. Not only my brethren and
myself, but likewise all the judges of England, think that without
this power no court could possibly exist ; nay, that no *contempt*
could indeed be committed against us, we should be *so truly con-
temptible.* The law upon the subject is of immemorial antiquity,
and there is not any period when it can be said to have ceased or
discontinued. On this point, therefore, we entertain no doubt."

These observations have since been repeatedly quoted as
conclusive on the subject of contempts ; and were cited with
approbation in the famous debate in January, 1818, in the case
of John Anderson in the house of representatives of the
United States.[3]

Lossing in his *Lives of the Signers*, referring to this matter,
says, "It was like ' the viper biting a file.' " And a late judge

---

[1] The impeachment resolution was chiefly defeated by the eloquence of
William Lewis.—*Brown's Forum.*

[2] Sanderson's *Lives.*

[3] Ibid.   Col. John Anderson attempted to bribe a member, and a long
debate ensued as to whether the House could punish him.   Joseph Hopkinson quoted a portion of the above paragraph.   See *Journals H. R.*, Fifteenth
Cong., 1st Sess.; also *Debates and Proceed.*, Gales and Seaton, 1854, Fifteenth
Cong., 1st Sess , pp. 722, 580 *et seq.*

of the Supreme Court, writing in *Hazard's Register of Penn-sylvania*,[1] on the Bench and Bar, says of Chief Justice Mc-Kean: "Many charges were made against him, finally, and attempts were made to impeach him; but all proved abortive, and only shed new lustre upon his character."

This is not the only instance in which the legislature at-tempted a wholesale impeachment of the Supreme Court for political purposes. Another case occurred in 1804, which will be noticed in its proper place.

PENNSYLVANIA CONSTITUTIONAL CONVENTION, 1789.

This Convention met on Tuesday, November 24, 1789, to frame a constitution for the State. It was at first proposed to reform the old constitution then in force, which was very defec-tive, with but a single legislative branch; but this was after-wards abandoned as hopeless. Judge McKean was a delegate from Philadelphia. Being resolved into committee of the whole, December 1st, in which the subject was chiefly discussed, Judge McKean was elected chairman. He therefore could not take part in the debates; he was, however, the author of the clause making provision for the establishment of schools throughout the States, so that the poor may be taught *gratis*. On his retirement from the chair January 29, 1790, he received a vote of thanks from the committee.[2]

MINOR MATTERS.

A few years before this, Judge McKean was appointed by Congress by a circuitous sort of ballot, one of nine judges to settle a certain territorial claim between the states of Georgia and South Carolina. James Madison and James Duane were among the judges chosen.[3]

Washington's birthday was celebrated in 1790 by the Soci-ety of the Cincinnati; and Chief Justice McKean did not think it beneath himself to march in procession with them through the streets.[4] On the 17th of April occurred the funeral of Benja-min Franklin. The pall-bearers on this occasion were, the President of the State, Thomas Mifflin; the Chief Justice, Thomas McKean; the President of the Bank, John Morton;

---

[1] iii., 241.
[2] Sanderson's *Lives*.
[3] *Journals*, Sept. 13, 1786.
[4] Scharf and Westcott, i., 463.

Samuel Powell, William Bingham, and David Rittenhouse, Esqs., accompanied by the city officers, militia, and others.[1] During this same year was organized the Hibernian Society for the relief of emigrants from Ireland. A number of benevolent gentlemen (among whom were several members of the Friendly Sons of St. Patrick, which society it superseded) met together on the 22d of March, and agreed upon a constitution, under which, on the 5th of April, the officers were elected, as follows : President, Hon. Thomas McKean ; Vice-President, General Walter Stewart ; Secretary, Matthew Carey : Treasurer, John Taylor ; with other subordinate officers. The society was incorporated under the laws of Pennsylvania, April 27, 1792, upon the petition of Thomas McKean and fifty-eight others. The records being imperfect from 1793 to 1813, it is not known how long Judge McKean served as president. The society is in a flourishing condition at the present day, being in possession of an investment fund of $70,000.[2]

In 1794 occurred what is known as the Whiskey Insurrection, in the Western part of Pennsylvania. Extreme coercion was about to be employed, and troops were called out by the general government, when Judge McKean suggested a mild and pacific course, which prevailed. Chief Justice McKean and General William Irvine were appointed commissioners on the part of the state; and James Ross, Judge Jasper Yeates and William Bradford (U. S. Attorney General), on the part of the United States.[3] On their way home after leaving Carlisle, two hundred men marched in, with the hope of catching Judge McKean and Judge Yeates, who was in his company ; but being disappointed in seizing the judges, burned them in effigy.[4] Of this great uprising, much has been written; there is a full account in the *Pennsylvania Colonial Records*, vol. iv, by Linn and Egle, 1876.

Towards the close of the year 1792 occurred the second presidential election, in which Chief Justice McKean took part as a presidential elector from the 3d Pennsylvania district. He cast his vote for Washington, who received the unanimous votes of all the electors, and who in due time entered upon his second term of office.[5]

---

[1] Ibid., i., 458 ; *Histor. Mag. of Notes and Queries*, i., 83–4.

[2] Pamphlets of the Society, 1887-9.

[3] *Hist. Whiskey Insurrection*, H. M. Breckenbridge, 1859, p. 190 ; also Egle's *Hist. Penn.*, i., 227.

[4] Hildrith's *U. S.*, iv., 505–11.

[5] Lanman's *Biog. Annals*.

WRITES A COMMENTARY ON THE CONSTITUTION.

During this same year, Thomas McKean and James Wilson published a work with the following title :

"Commentary on the Constitution of the United States of America, with that Constitution prefixed, in which are unfolded the Principles of free Government; and the superior Advantages of Republicanism demonstrated." By James Wilson, LL. D., and Thomas McKean, LL. D. T. Lloyd. 8vo., pp. 147. 3 s. Debret, 1792.

Both of the authors were signers of the Declaration, and they had been the two principal leaders in the convention which ratified the constitution. McKean was Chief Justice, and Wilson an associate justice of the Supreme Court. Wilson was also at that time professor of law in the University of Pennsylvania. This work was favorably commented upon by that standard publication, the *London Monthly Review* for October, 1792 (iii, 155), which concludes as follows :

"The publication must be perused throughout in order to form an idea of the good sense, and manly eloquence of the speeches here made public.[1]

COMMOTIONS CAUSED BY JAY'S TREAY.

The revolution which dethroned Louis XVI now broke out in France, and England with other countries declared war against her. Very naturally the popular sympathy in the United States was with France our old ally, and against England our late enemy. Assistance to France was proposed by many ; and opposed by others, who raised the objection that the country had no resources, and was as yet but feebly established. To avert a war, a secret treaty with England was concluded by John Jay at London, November 19, 1794. On being made public in June following, a few days after its ratification by the Senate, (June 24th,) it was received at first with an almost united roar of execration throughout the land.[2] Public meetings in various places gave expression to the feeling against it.

In Philadelphia a meeting was held July 24th, at which Dr. William Shippen presided. Governor Mifflin, Chief Justice McKean, Frederick A. Muhlenberg, David Rittenhouse, Alex-

---

[1] See also *Penn. Mag.*, xi., 271 ; Allibone's *Dict. of Authors*, art. *McKean.*
[2] Randall's *Thomas Jefferson*, iii., 258–65–66.

ander J. Dallas, Charles Pettit, Thomas Lee Shippen, Jared Ingersol, Blair McClenachan and others were mounted on a stage and favored war with England. The treaty was read, and then contemptuously thrown off the stage. It was caught up by a crowd, who marched with it to the house of the British Minister and to Senator William Bingham's, where the treaty was publicly burned.[1] Nevertheless the treaty was proclaimed and war averted,—happily so for the country. John Adams, who favored the other side of the question, referred to this matter in a letter to Thomas McKean dated June 2, 1812, as follows: "Nearly thirty-eight years ago our friendship commenced. It has never been interrupted to my knowledge but by one event."[2] Their friendship however after that event continued unbroken to the end.

A PRESIDENTIAL ELECTOR.

At the third presidential election in 1796 Adams and Jefferson were the two principal competitors. Chief Justice McKean headed the republican list of Presidential Electors in Pennsylvania, being one of the two electors at large,—the second time he had filled this position. Pennsylvania was entitled to fifteen electors, and among those from the congressional districts, were Joseph Hiester afterwards Governor, General William Irvine, Colonel Samuel Miles, and Peter Muhlenberg.[3] This ticket, which favored Thomas Jefferson, was elected, received 12,306 votes in the state, against 12,181 for the whig ticket headed by Whelen, which favored Mr. Adams.[4] At the election, Mr. Jefferson received fourteen of the fifteen votes. Mr. Adams however had a majority of the whole number cast and was elected president.

HEATED POLITICAL AFFAIRS. PETER PORCUPINE'S LAWSUITS.

Politics still continued to agitate the people, the newspapers being not the least of the causes, which kept up the excitement. William Duane of the *Aurora* was particularly abusive in all his writings. At length, as we may read in McMaster's

---

[1] Ibid., and Scharf and Westcott, i., 475–81.
[2] *Works*, by his grandson, C. F. Adams, 1856, x., 13, and Sanderson's *Lives*.
[3] Lanman, *Biog. Annals*, p. 514.
[4] Scharf and Westcott, i., 485.

History,[1] weary of this abuse, a number of militiamen, led by Joseph B. McKean, son of the Chief Justice, one afternoon in May waited on the editor, and demanded an apology. Mr. Duane refused; whereupon he was seized, dragged down stairs, and flogged in the public street. For this chastisement, Duane entered suit against Joseph B. McKean and thirty others; but they were acquitted after the suit had hung on for several years.[2]

Notwithstanding this, Duane took sides with Judge McKean in his canvass for governor; but like many politicians turned against him eventually. His wholesale abuse brought him continually into trouble. In February, just before the episode above related, he became involved in a quarrel with the congregation of St. Mary's church; and together with Dr. James Reynolds was arrested and brought before the mayor. Judge McKean appeared in their behalf, much to the dissatisfaction of the opposite party.[3]

Duane continued his abuse, and the opinion with which he was regarded by the opposition may be seen from the following extract from the *Federalist or New Jersey Gazette*, August 5, 1799. "On Tuesday last, Duane the infamous Aurora man was arrested by the marshall of the district of Pennsylvania upon a warrant from Judge Peters, for publishing in the Aurora of the 24th *ultimo*, a gross and virulent libel upon the government of the United States." The libel, the editor then goes on to say, was, that in 1798, the British government distributed $800,000 among officers of the United States as secret service money.

There was another also who took part in the politics of these times, so distinguished as a writer that he deserves more than a passing notice; and that person is William Cobbett, whose ready and sarcastic pen kept him ever in trouble. He was the editor of a weekly paper,--*The Gazette*, and wrote under the pseudonym of *Peter Porcupine*.[4]

---

[1] *Hist. People of U. S.*, ii., 439.

[2] Scharf and Westcott, i., 497, 533.

[3] Scharf and Westcott, i., 497. Also *Wharton's State Trials of the U. S.*, 1849, p. 345.

[4] He was born in England in 1762, came to Philadelphia, and edited *Porcupine's Gazette*, in which he attacked and slandered almost every one; thereby becoming involved in suits for slander without number. Of all the opponents of Thomas McKean during his exciting canvass for Governor, Cobbett was the most rancorous. He "boasted of having immortalized the Governor in every country where the English language is spoken." (*Loy-*

84	MCKEAN FAMILY.

In this paper in 1797, Cobbett slandered the Spanish Minister, Señor Martinez de Yrujo, and the Spanish King, calling the former, whom he nicknamed Don Yarico, a fop, half don and half sans-culotte; and the latter a poor degraded creature. For this, Señor Martinez de Yrujo complained against Cobbett, and he was bound over in the District Court charged as a common libeller; but broke his conditions and the cause then came in the Supreme Court before Chief Justice McKean. The defendant petitioned to have his case transferred to the Circuit Court; but the Supreme Court rejected it. Chief Justice McKean presided at the trial.[1] "His charge to the jury was a fine one. His explication of the law of libel did him credit," says McMaster[2] the historian, but adds that the Chief Justice turned libeller upon the prisoner at the bar. Cobbett was acquitted by a single vote, (10 to 9.) It is stated in the Life of Cobbett, that Chief Justice McKean then determined to suppress Cobbett's wholesale abuse, and collecting a number of his pamphlets, compelled him on his own authority as Chief Justice to go under bonds to keep the peace, and be of good behavior.[3] Cobbett, in his inimitable style, relates this in a letter to Dr. Joseph Priestly, as follows[4]—

" He then collected a bundle of my pamphlets and papers, and thereupon issued a warrant, . . . [which] stated that I had published

alist *Poetry of the Revolution.* p. 171.) After McKean's election he sailed for England, and it was thought that he would favor the royalist side, since he had opposed the republican form of government in America; but no, his pen at once turned against the king and ministry, and he was soon convicted of various libels against the government and individuals, fined and imprisoned. By one of those strange freaks of fortune, he was elected to Parliament, but failed signally in that sphere, making several blunders. Allibone says that in Parliament he "roared as gently as any sucking dove." Southey declared that "As an author he stands very high; there never was a better or more forcible writer. In public he seemed almost against every - one." (*New Am. Encycl.*) Judgments of the courts against him for damages he deemed as robbery; Parliament he considered little better than a mob for laughing him down. So even in his *Grammar of the English Language* (Letter xvii., § 181) he cannot conceal his sarcasm, as the following singular extract will show : " Nouns of number or multitude, such as Mob, Parliament, Rabble, House of Commons, Regiment, Court of King's Bench, Den of Thieves, and the like, may have pronouns agreeing with them either in the singular or plural number." See his Life, "How to Get on in the World," Robert Waters, N., Y., 1883.

[1] 3 *Dallas*, 467, December term, 1798; also reprinted in *State Trials of the U. S.*, Francis Wharton, LL. D., Phila., 1849.

[2] *Hist. of People of U. S.*, 1855, ii., 353.

[3] *How to Get on in the World*, R. Waters, N. Y., 1883, p. 60.

[4] *The Rush Light*, Cobbett's Works, xi., 427.

certain false and malicious libels against himself, Mifflin, Dallas, Jefferson, Munroe, Gallatin, old Franklin, the Duke of Bedford, Charles Fox, Sheridan, Lord Stanhope, Bonaparte, the Bishop of Bergamo, Pichegru, Robespierré, Talleyrand, Parker the mutineer, Napper Tandy, Arthur O'Conner,—and the devil knows who besides."

ELECTED GOVERNOR OF PENNSYLVANIA.

In October 1799, after a furious political contest with James Ross, Thomas McKean was elected Governor of Pennsylvania. There were two political parties: the *Republican* or *Demo-cratic-Republican*, (a term which came into use about this time,) and the Federalist. The former, which was against the encroachments of the federal government, supported McKean; the latter, which favored the strong measures of the government, voted for Ross.[1] McKean received 38,036 votes against 32,643 for Ross, a majority of 5393 ;[2] The election marked an important era in politics ; for it brought in power the new party which was afterwards destined to rule the country for many years.

HIS ELECTION OPPOSED BY COBBETT.

One of the most bitter opponents of Thomas McKean in the canvass for governor was William Cobbett. He had never forgiven the Chief Justice for his decisions in those previous lawsuits, and now his aggravating sarcasm, his great fluency of expression, and his pointed and undisguised statements, made him an opponent by no means to be despised. But the acrimony of the contest having long since passed away, an account of his attacks cannot fail to be interesting, but will doubtless now provoke merely a smile from the reader of these pages. The author does not guarantee the truth of the statements quoted ; but that may also be a feature of Cobbett's style :

"*Judge McKean :* This vile old wretch who now disgraces the courts of the unfortunate State of Pennsylvania, was formerly a stable-man at a tavern in Chester county. The following lines allude to his state of innocence :

" OLD TOPER, to *currying horses* was bred,
But tir'd of so humble a life,

---

[1] *Life of Thomas Jefferson*, Henry S. Randall, ii., 506.
[2] *Legis. Handbook of Pa.*, T. B. Cochran, 1889, for the votes in detail ; Scharf and Westcott, i., 498 ; see also Hildrith's *U. S.*, v., 314. Hildrith gives the votes each 10,000 too small.

To *currying favor* he turned his head,
And 's now *curried* himself by his wife."[1]

In another place, with great sarcasm, he says :

"His [McKean's] grandfather was an Irishman who emigrated with the consent of his majesty and twelve good and true men."[2]

It would be strange if Cobbett's abuse should overreach itself and turn in McKean's favor. Can it be that Cobbett here, with a little confusion of generations, alludes to the Claverhouse jury mentioned in the Introduction ? If so, it settles the matter in the affirmative that the Pennsylvania and the New England McKeans have the same origin.

In regard to naturalizing foreigners, no one ever represented the matter in such a light as Cobbett in the following sentence :

"McKean. This *honorable* personage is not only canvassing as he goes his circuit (gracious God !), he is not only soliciting votes of the *present citizens*, but he is absolutely *making new ones*."[3]

Accusing McKean of trying to conciliate the Quakers whom he offended by the execution of Roberts and Carlisle, Cobbett writes :

"'Now by St. Paul the work goes bravely on ! !' Nothing that I ever saw or ever heard of would please me half so well as to see 'The Honor, the Doctor of Laws, Esqr.,' in a broad-brimmed hat and a cape coat. But halt ! What shall we do with the three tailed wig ? It must not hang dangling down over a piece of smooth mouse-colored cloth ; and as to *a cap*, it would never suit either a judge or a governor. A red liberty cap, indeed, some governors have been proud to wear ; but this, I take it, would suit worse with a Quaker coat than even a three tailed wig. Notwithstanding this difficulty, however, I sincerely hope the conversion will take place.[4]

About this time Cobbett turned his attention to Dr. Rush, charging that he bled his patients to death. Finally Rush sued him, and the case came before Chief Justice McKean, governor elect, but still in the bench, and Judge Shippen. Shippen then came in for his share of abuse, as well also as the counsel engaged, namely, Joseph Hopkinson (son of the signer and author of " Hail Columbia"), and Edward J. Coale (men

---

[1] *Porcupine's Works,* by William Cobbett, London, 1801, 12 vols., vii., 300, *Gazette Selections.*

[2] Ibid., vii., 333.

[3] Ibid., x., 206.

[4] Ibid., x., 212.

tioned elsewhere in this genealogy), a relative of Hopkinson, and a student in his office. Dr. Rush got a verdict of $5000.[1]

Finally, when the election drew nigh, with every prospect of McKean's success, Cobbett became so wrought up that he published the following threat:

"I *know* McKean, and I know that it is my duty, my bounded duty to my subscribers in this state, to use all my feeble efforts to preserve them from the power of such a man. From private considerations, there is no man who need care less about the issue of the election than myself. It is out of McKean's power to hurt me. *I will never live six months under his sovereign sway.*"[2]

True to his threat, on the news of the election of McKean, Cobbett prepared to leave Philadelphia; but was not able to do so before execution was levied by Dr. Rush and others on his personal effects that swept away nearly all his property.[3]

He inserted in the *Federalist or New Jersey Gazette* of December 16, 1799, the following advertisement:

"WILLIAM COBBETT having, (in order to avoid the disgrace of living under the Government of MacKean,) removed from Philadelphia to New York, requests all those who may have occasion to write to him, to direct their letters to the latter city, No. 141 Water street."

On his arrival in New York he published the following card (January 1800):

"To the subscribers of this Gazette: Remembering as you must my solemn promise to quit Pennsylvania, in case my old democratic Judge MACK KEAN should be elected Governor; and knowing as you now do that he is elected to that office, there are, I trust, very few of you who will be surprised to find that I am no longer in that degraded and degrading state."[4]

He published the *Rush Light* in New York for a while, in which he continued his abuse on Rush, McKean, Shippen, Hopkinson, and Harper; and ended by consigning all Philadelphians to perdition, and sailed for Europe.[5]

The democratic-republicans went wild over the election of Thomas McKean, for it was the first triumph of the new party. Addresses were made to him, in various places; and banquets given, in which he was toasted. In the Aurora of November

---

[1] Ibid., xi., 360–3.
[2] Ibid., x., 190.
[3] Scharf and Westcott, i., 497.
[4] *Cobbett's Works,* xi., 137.
[5] Scharf and Westcott, i., 499.

9th, appeared one of the party songs, which concluded as follows:

The day of election the Tories regret,
Five thousand and odd 's a majority great;
So here 's to the health of Republican Green
And Republican Blue and old Thomas McKean.

On the 6th of November, at a town meeting held in Philadelphia, an address was prepared congratulating the governor-elect upon his success. To this, Judge McKean replied that under his administration their happy system of government, raised on the sole authority of the people, would, he trusted, by the favor of God, be continued inviolate; that neither foreign nor domestic enemies, neither intrigue, menace, nor seductions should prevail against it; and that the constitution of the United States and of Pennsylvania, should be the rule of his government.[1] The reply created some stir at the time, on account of its strong partisan language, and it was afterwards brought up against him.[2]

TAKES THE OATH OF OFFICE.   HIS REMOVALS FROM OFFICE.

Judge McKean took the oath of office as governor on the 17th of December, 1799. In the *Federalist*, or New Jersey Gazette, of December 23d, 1799, is the announcement that McKean was proclaimed Governor of Pennsylvania on the 18th instant,[3] also that Edward Shippen is appointed Chief Justice, and Hugh H. Brackenridge, of Pittsburg, a Judge of the Supreme Court. This paper is deeply edged with black, as it contains the announcement of the lamented decease of General Washington.

As soon as Governor McKean entered upon his duties, he began a series of removals from office, of various persons, high and low, which he deemed for the public good. In a letter to John Dickinson, June 23, 1800, he says: "I have waded through a sea troubles, and surmounted my principal difficulties. I have been obliged (though no Hercules), *to cleanse the Augean stable*, with little or no aid; for I am my own minister and amanuensis."[4]

Governor McKean, as might be expected, was attacked by

[1] Sanderson's *Lives*.
[2] Scharf and Westcott, i., 504.
[3] A mistake for 17th.
[4] Sanderson's *Lives*, where a lengthy defense of these removals is entered into. In some of the volumes of *Penn. Senate Journal* may be found long lists of the Governor's appointments, 1805–6–7, and thereabouts.

his political opponents, and his course ascribed wholly to political antagonism. Alexander Graydon was one of those removed by him. He was performing the duties of prothonotary of Dauphin county "until his sudden expulsion by McKean, to whom," he says, "belongs the unenviable distinction of being the father of political proscription in the United States."[1] Charles Biddle, also a contemporary, says of the Governor, " I knew he was very much provoked at some severe pieces, written against him by my nephew, Mr. Marks John Biddle. However, Governor McKean and myself had always been upon good terms, and I had a high esteem for him, believing him to be a very honest man, although a very violent one, who had no command of his temper; but spoke whatever he thought upon all occasions." Although Mr. Graydon, who was remotely connected with the governor by marriage, was turned out of office, yet Biddle was retained, though he had every expectation of being removed.[2]

His political enemies, the Federalists, berated Governor McKean, as may be seen from the two following extracts from *The Administrations of Washington and Adams—the Federal Administrations :*[3] " After all, McKean is a better governor than Mifflin. He won't corrupt society more, if as much, and the work he does will be more open." (Letter of Chauncey Goodrich, Hartford, Nov. 18, 1799.) " McKean's administration has brought forward every scoundrel who can read and write, into office or expectation of one, and the residue of Democrats, with the joy and precocity of the damned, are enjoying the mortification of the few remaining honest men and Federalists." (Letter of Uriah Tracy, Pittsburg, Aug. 7, 1800.)

" Mr. McKean's gubernatorial career," says a recent biographer," was marked by great ability, and produced beneficial results to the commonwealth. He was a rigid partisan, well disciplined in tactics, a devout believer in the Jeffersonian maxim that, ' to the victors belong the spoils.' In carrying out his specific views of this theory, his wholesale removals of political opponents was unprecedented in our early history."[4]

The Federalists in the legislature now attacked Governor McKean for his speech on the 6th of November, as well as for his removals. It was moved in the House of Representatives

---

[1] *Memoirs of His Own Time*, 1846, p. xiii.

[2] *Autobiog. Ch. Biddle*, by Craig Biddle, 1883, p. 383.

[3] *Geo. Gibbs*, 2 vols., N. Y., 1846, ii., 288, 399.

[4] Nevin, *Continental Sketches of Distinguished Pennsylvanians*, 1875.

90   McKEAN FAMILY.

to condemn him, but that branch containing a majority of
Democrats, the vote was lost.[1] The Senate, however, passed a
resolution condemning him, to which he made a long reply,
" declaring that the objectionable expressions were uttered
before he assumed office ; and that as regarded his removals
from office, he relied upon his right to make such changes as
he deemed proper without accountability to any person or
party,"[2]—a reply characteristic of his firmness of purpose in
what he believed to be right.

His object in removing opponents was not to make places
merely for political friends, but to secure efficiency and har-
mony to his rule.   For when the affairs of his administration
once became settled on a firm basis, he did not adhere exclu-
sively to his own party in making appointments.   He twice
elevated to the highest position in his power to bestow, that of
chief justice of the state, gentlemen whose political views were
adverse to his own.[3]

In verification of this statement, the following anecdote may
properly find a place here.   When Tilghman was nominated
for chief justice, a committee was sent, who announced themselves as representing the sovereign people, the great democ-
racy of Philadelphia, and declaring that they could never ap-
prove this nomination.   The governor listened with his usual
haughty courtesy, and bowing profoundly, replied, " Inform
your constituents that I bow with submission to the great de-
mocracy of Philadelphia ; but, by God ! William Tilghman
shall be chief justice of Pennsylvania."   *And he was.*[4]   He
received his appointment February 28, 1806.

Another anecdote is related, of an appointment which cannot be charged to political reasons.   A very worthy man
(John Goodman) applied to him for a commission as justice of
the peace ; but stated very frankly that he had no certificates
or backers.   " Never mind," said the Governor, " I require
none ; and if any one should ask you how you got your appointment, tell him that Thomas McKean recommended you,
and the Governor appointed you."[5]

Not long after this, Governor McKean removed his nephew
by marriage, Joseph Hopkinson, and appointed John Beckley

[1] Scharf and Westcott, i., 504.
[2] Egle, *Illust. Hist. of Penn.*, i., 234–5.
[3] Armor, *Lives of Govs. of Penn.*, p. 303 ; see also Sanderson's *Lives.*
[4] R. H. Davis, in *Harp. Mag.*, lii., 872.
[5] David Paul Brown, *The Forum*, i., 345.

to the office. A controversy ensued over this in which Joseph B. McKean appeared in behalf of his father. Governor McKean was also assailed for participating as Grand Sachem at an anniversary celebration of the St. Tammany Society, May 12, 1800, at Buck Tavern, Moyamensing. The ceremony was burlesqued in the *Phila. Gazette* of June 2d, 1800.[1]

Next President Adams made an appointment which set in motion a lively controversy. He appointed Alexander J. Dallas district attorney, which gave dissatisfaction, as Dallas was already Secretary of the Commonwealth. He resigned the latter, and Governor McKean appointed him Recorder of Philadelphia. The common council objected to this, as he held two offices. Proceedings were had and the case was argued by Hopkinson, Lewis and Tilghman for the councils, and by Joseph B. McKean and Ingersoll for Dallas. The defendants (Dallas) won the case, and the legislature at the next session took up the matter and passed a law prohibiting a person from holding both state and federal offices. Governor McKean vetoed this, as he could not admit thereby that he had done any wrong in appointing Dallas as Recorder. The House passed the bill over his veto and Dallas resigned.[2] It is readily seen that the root of this controversy was, that the law or custom of holding more than one office, was not then well defined, as it is now; and such cases as the above-related, assisted materially in settling the law and custom.

In justification of Governor McKean's removals from office, I know of no stronger argument, than that which may be drawn from the writings of his opponents themselves. I will first cite William Cobbett, in regard to the dilemma of Governor Mifflin's appointees to office:[3]

"Two candidates offered, Ross and McKean. In the latter they remembered indeed the old revolutionist; but they also remembered that he was not a Mifflin. Keen, vigilant, persevering, tyrannical and vindictive as they knew McKean to be, they were afraid to give him their support lest they should have him for a master; and afraid to oppose him lest they should be displaced. Being at last fully persuaded that Ross would succeed, they openly gave him their support. They were egregiously deceived. McKean was elected by a vast majority; and though his great age was one of the objections they affected to have against

[1] Scharf and Westcott, i., 504.
[2] Ibid., i., 509.
[3] *Works*, xi., 387.

him, he soon made them feel that he was not deficient in point
of energy.

"The first step he took was to annul all commissions during
pleasure, granted by his predecessor. He had previously obtained
exact information respecting the electioneering conduct of every
one of the civil officers, whom he had power to displace ; and according to this, he made out his list of proscription. He swept
the poor fellows off by dozens, with as little ceremony as a foul
feeding glutton brushes the flies from the meat he is himself going
to devour."

Had Governor McKean transcended his legitimate powers
one iota, or overstepped the law in the smallest particular,
would not Cobbett have eagerly seized upon it? The fact
that Cobbett does not bring such a charge is circumstantial evidence that Governor McKean did not overstep the laws in his
removals. He first annulled the commissions " *during pleasure ;*" he then made a list of those " *whom he had power to
displace.*" He had a clear right to remove these two classes.
As to the office holders, Cobbett depicts them in an unenviable
light, weak, unreliable and insincere to either candidate, thinking solely how to retain their offices. The removals are thus
seen to be not contrary to *law*, although contrary to custom.

The letter of Chauncey Goodrich, quoted a few pages back,
says, " the work he does will be more open," thus testifying
that Governor McKean's work is not done in secret or in the
dark, but is open to the criticism of his adversaries. The
other letter quoted contains abuse, but nothing against McKean
more than its language is against its own author. Cobbett's
attacks, as may be seen from the extracts given, were generally
abuse, or ridicule, that may have influenced some at that time.
Such evanescent attacks contain but little to influence posterity.

The photolithographed *fac-simile* of a printed hand-bill on
the opposite page, is given as a curious memento of these tur-
bulent times. It has been preserved in the family, and is now
in possession of the author. The photolithograph is reduced
two-thirds of the original size.[1]

The news that the presidential election between Jefferson
and Burr had resulted in a tie, was known towards the close of
the year 1800, and much elated the democratic republicans,
as the election would then be thrown into the House of Representatives. Meetings, festivals, and banquets were held in

---

[1] The paper is torn and the print worn away in places. It is not known
who wrote the line at the bottom.

BY DESIRE OF

GOVERNOR M'KEAN,

Who means to honor the Theatre with his prefence,

THIS EVENING, January 2, 1800,

At the Houfe of Mr. LENEGAN, in Eaft King-ftreet, Lancafter,

At the Sign of the White Horfe.

———:◉:———

 Ͳᴴᴱ LADIES & GENTLEMEN of Lancafter are ref-
pectfully informed, that this evening will be prefent-
ed the greateft variety of amufements that has ever
been exhibited in this town, confifting of

Pantomime, Singing, Hornpipe *Danc-ing,* Tumbling, SPEAKING, &c. &c.

And in particular an Indian WAR and SCALP Dance,
by Mr. Durang and Mr. F. Ricketts.

Doors to be opened at fix and the performance to begin at 7 o'clock.
Tickets to be had at Mr, Lenegan's and at Hamilton's Printing-Office.

LADIES and GENTLEMEN who wifh to engage feats may have
calling upon Mr. Rowson at the Theatre.

ROWSON & Co.

Printed by William Hamilton, King-ftreet, Lancafter.

NB one Box was appropriated and occupied by the Governor,

various places, among which was a splendid gathering at the Green Tree Tavern at Philadelphia to hear speeches, drink toasts, and sing "Jefferson and Liberty," till they were hoarse. One stanza of this favorite party song ran as follows:

> Calumny and falsehood in vain raise their voice
> To blast our Republican's fair reputation;
> But Jefferson still is America's fair choice,
> And he will, her liberties, guard from invasion.
> 'Tis the wretches who wait,
> To unite church and state,
> That the names of McKean, Burr, and
>   Jefferson hate.
> But ne'er will the sons of Columbia be slaves,
> While the earth bears a plant, or the sea rolls its waves.[1]

SECOND ELECTION AS GOVERNOR.

In the fall of 1802, Governor McKean was re-elected; his popularity gaining for him an immense majority, receiving no less than 47,879 votes, against 17,037 for his old competitor Ross. His majority was 30,000 in a total vote of 65,000.[2] Is not this majority alone a vindication of his three years administration? *Three-fourths* of the people of the state are with him. The opposition is headed by a mere faction, which however makes a great noise. Politics ran exceedingly high at this election also. A banquet was given to the Governor at Hamburg Tavern, and also at Francis' Union Hall. And a procession to celebrate the acquisition of Louisiana laid out the route of the march to pass the Governor's house on Third street, May 12, 1804.[3]

During this year (1804) occurred the Brackenridge episode. The legislature was acting on a matter of the impeachment of three of the four judges of the supreme court, for alleged arbitrary conduct in committing to prison for contempt of court, one of the parties in a suit then pending; the contempt consisted in an abusive publication in the newspapers. The case was similar to that of Oswald already related in these pages. Judge Brackenridge the fourth judge happened to be absent, and was not embraced in the impeachment; he how-ever. sent a letter to the assembly, that he concurred in the

[1] McMaster's *U. S.*, ii., 512.

[2] *Legislative Handbook of Pa.*, Cochran, 1889, p. 398; Hildrith's *U. S.*, v., 466; Adams' *Works*, x., 121; Scharf and Westcott, i., 513.

[3] Scharf and Westcott, i., 513–19.

7

course taken by the other judges.[1] For this, the legislature sent an address to the Governor requesting his removal; but the request was utterly refused. The committee attempted to remonstrate with him, stating that the expression " *may* remove" in the address was equivalent to " *must* remove." Governor McKean heard them patiently ; and bowing, replied, " I will have you know, gentlemen, that *May* sometimes means *Won't*.[2]

This was not the only instance in which the legislature attempted to interfere with the governor's prerogative, or to instruct him in his duties, neither of which would he allow ; and on another occasion, a committee of the legislature fared no better than the previous had done.

The governor having vetoed what was deemed an important bill passed by the legislature, a committee of three of that body was appointed to wait upon his excellency to remonstrate with him, and to urge the reconsideration of his veto. He received them with his accustomed dignified politeness, and after they had explained their mission, apparently without noticing their communication, he deliberately took out his watch, and handing it to the chairman, said, " Pray, sir, look at my watch; she has been out of order for some time ; will you please put her to rights ?" " Sir," replied the chairman, with some surprise, " I am no watchmaker ; I am a carpenter." The watch was then handed to the other members of the committee, both of whom declined, one being a currier, and the other a bricklayer. " Well," said the governor, " this is truly strange! Any watchmaker's apprentice can repair that watch; it is a simple piece of mechanism, and yet you can't do it! The law, gentlemen, is a science of great difficulty and endless complication; it requires a life-time to understand it. I have bestowed a quarter of a century upon it; yet *you*, who can't mend this little watch, become *lawyers all at once*, and presume to instruct me in my duty." Of course the committee vanished.[3]

In 1804 an act was passed to substitute referees for a jury, thinking that if trials by jury could be gotten rid of, lawyers might be dispensed with. Governor McKean vetoed this bill, and thereupon sprang up between him and the Assembly a violent quarrel, which presently reached a great height. Mc-

[1] Hildrith's *U. S.*, v., 514.

[2] David Paul Brown, *The Forum*, where the year is given wrongly 1806 ; Scharf and Westcott, i., 517.

[3] *The Forum*, i., 344.

Kean was assailed by his old ally Duane, whose chief sup-porter was Michael Leib.[1]

A historical writer of a series of biographical articles in the *Village Record*, of West Chester, Pennsylvania (Sept. 8, 1860), with but little apparent partiality to Governor McKean, gives a sketch of his life, laying particular stress on the con-troversy with General Thompson, the address of December 6th, etc., and concludes as follows: "It is curious to remark that before the second term . . . he quarreled with his old friends, and threw himself into the arms of the politicians so graphi-cally mentioned in the response above quoted, by whom he was triumphantly sustained for a third term."

SOLICITED TO BECOME A CANDIDATE FOR VICE PRESIDENT OF THE UNITED STATES.

The early growth of the Republican or Democratic party, has already been noted in these pages. Let us recapitulate. In 1796, McKean, then chief justice, headed the presidential ticket as an elector-at-large. In Pennsylvania the party was successful; but Jefferson was not elected president. Three years after, McKean was elected governor by a large majority. His popularity vastly increased during his term of office ; and this, added to his great personal and political influence, con-tributed in no small degree to the election of Mr. Jefferson to the presidency the succeeding year.[2] And during the whole of that gentleman's administration, the weight of Governor McKean's opinions and conduct was directed to upholding the principles which marked the policy of the general government.[3]

Then followed Governor McKean's immense majority at his re-election, which brought him forward as one of the most prominent men in his party. Being a strong candidate, he was, therefore, in the fall of 1803, urgently solicited to become a candidate for the Vice-Presidency with Mr. Jefferson at his second nomination. Alexander J. Dallas[4] thus addresses him on this subject, under date of October 14th, 1803:

---

[1] Hildrith's *U. S.*, v., 514.

[2] Nevin, *Continental Sketches of Distinguished Pennsylvanians;* Sanderson's *Lives;* Goodrich's *Lives*, etc.

[3] Sanderson's *Lives*.

[4] Without an especial mention of this gentleman, the warm personal and political friend of Governor McKean, this biography would be incomplete. Alexander James Dallas was born in the island of Jamaica in 1759, of a Scottish family. He removed to Philadelphia, was admitted to the bar, and took a high stand in his profession ; published the laws of Pennsylvania,

" I have been requested by several of our friends, to bear with
me (to Washington,) your sentiments as to the office of vice-
president. Your name has been most honorably mentioned on the
occasion. Pray write me, in perfect confidence, and address your
letter to the care of Mr. Gallatin, at Washington. Accustomed
as I have been for many years, to wish every thing that can pro-
mote your happiness or reputation, it would give me pain to find,
that in this instance, your disposition should lead you to the federal scene : as I do not believe there exists another man in Pennsylvania, to whom, at this period, the real interests of the state
can be safely confided. But your choice will entirely govern my
opinions and expressions."[1]

Governor McKean declined this honor both on public and
private considerations. Had he accepted, he would assuredly
have been elected, as George Clinton of New York was then
nominated, and chosen with Mr. Jefferson at his second election in 1804.

About this time it was reported that Governor McKean
"has been appointed minister plenipotentiary to the court of
Madrid, to adjust existing difficulties relative to the possessions
of Louisiana." Whether he was offered the position, or
whether it was a mere rumor, cannot now be ascertained.[2]

THIRD ELECTION AS GOVERNOR—VIRULENT PARTY FEELING—
IMPEACHMENT PROCEEDINGS.

In the fall of 1805, as the time for election approached,
Duane, Leib, and other political enemies of McKean organized
in secret;[3] and founded societies throughout the state to pre-
vent his nomination. They issued an address to the public,
setting forth McKean's " austerity, and aristocratic habits,"
his " years of professional contention and dominion in courts ;"
his "ungracious distribution of offices among relatives," and

and was subsequently reporter of the Supreme Court of the United States.
He was Secretary of State of Pennsylvania for several terms, both before
and during Governor McKean's administration. He was also U. S. District
Attorney, and in 1814 was appointed Secretary of the Treasury. He proved
to be an able and energetic officer during trying financial times following
the war of 1812. Besides being a law writer, he was also an author of
various works. He died in 1817, leaving two sons who became prominent,
Commodore A. J. Dallas, U. S. Navy ; and the Hon. George M. Dallas, Vice-
President of the United States 1845-9 ; and a daughter, who was the wife
of Judge William Wilkins, Senator and Secretary of War.—*Appleton.*

[1] Sanderson's *Lives.*

[2] *Balt. Gazette and Daily Adv.*, Nov. 3, 1803.

[3] Mark the contrast : we read above that McKean's acts are done openly.

his present intimacy "with those who had been his former libelers." The federalists, knowing it to be impossible to elect one of their own party, and hoping to break McKean's majority, nominated a *democrat;* but McKean's popularity was too great for defeat, and he was successfully elected over Simon Snyder, by a large majority—nearly 5000 votes.[1] The senate and house were strongly for McKean.

The Governor thus vindicated, began separate lawsuits against John Steele, William Dickson, Matthew Lawler, Thomas Leiper, Dr. Leib, Jacob Mitchell, and William Duane, publisher of the *Aurora,* for various publications and utterances.[2]

In July, 1806, the Governor appointed Dr. George Buchanan, of Baltimore, his son-in-law, lazaretto physician. Dr. Buchanan had for seventeen years been a citizen and resident of Baltimore, not arriving in Pennsylvania until just before the appointment was made. This appointment created some stir; and the *Aurora,* under the title of *"The Royal Family,"* gave the following list of persons connected by blood or marriage with the family of the Governor, who held office in the State:

Thomas McKean, Governor.

Joseph B. McKean, son, Attorney-General.

Thomas McKean, Jr., son, Private Secretary.

Thomas McKean Thompson, nephew, Secretary of Commonwealth.

Andrew Pettit, son-in-law, Flour Inspector.

Andrew Bayard, brother-in-law to Pettit, Auctioneer.

Dr. George Buchanan, son-in-law, Lazaretto Physician.

William McKennan, brother in-law of T. McKean Thompson, Prothonotary of Washington county.

Andrew Henderson, cousin to the Governor, Prothonotary of Huntingdon county.

William Henderson, cousin to the Governor, Brigade Inspector of Huntingdon county.

John Huested, father-in-law of T. McKean Thompson, clerk in the Comptroller General's office.

Joseph Reed, a near relative to Pettit and Bayard, Prothonotary of the Supreme Court.

[The term "connected by blood or marriage," is considerably stretched to make up the above list. Besides the Governor, only three are *near* relations and two connections.]

---

[1] *Leg. Handbook of Pa.,* Cochran, 1889, p. 398; Scharf and Westcott, i., 519. See also Randall's *Thomas Jefferson,* iii., 135; Hildrith's *United States,* v. 556.

[2] Scharf and Westcott, i., 520.

98   McKEAN FAMILY.

Even before the list was published, the *Aurora* was being
sued by the Governor on three libel cases, and by the Marquis
de Casa Yrujo, another son-in-law, on three more charges.
Before the close of July, Duane was the defendant in sixty or
seventy libel suits; and kept the staid old city in a turmoil,
wondering what he would publish next.[1]

Governor McKean continued to make many removals from
office, and his appointment of William Tilghman, a federalist,
as already related on a previous page, gave offense to many of
his own party. In April he added to the quarrel by attending
a dinner of the St. George's Society, where the health of the
king was drunk. About this time (November), the grand
jury of the mayor's court indicted Duane for publishing a toast
given at a celebration, " General Arnold and Governor Mc-
Kean, both beans of one kidney."

In the beginning of 1807, politics continued to agitate the
state with undiminished activity. The virulence of the opposition to General McKean took every conceivable shape. Representatives Leib and Engle desired a committee to investigate
his conduct, but the motion was lost. On the 19th of March,
Governor McKean, through Joseph B. McKean, Attorney-
General, tried to have Michael Leib and William Duane arrested for conspiracy, but the Supreme Court refused the
warrant. In May, Thomas McKean, Jr., who the previous
autumn had challenged Dr. Leib, was arrested, and in October
the grand jury found indictments against both McKean and his
second, Major Dennis.[2]

Dr. Michael Leib, mentioned above, had been a member of
Congress, but resigned his seat there, especially to put himself
at the head of his party in the Pennsylvania Assembly, and
oppose Governor McKean.[3]

It is probable that no public man in this country, excepting
Washington, so deeply involved in public affairs as Governor
McKean, has ever kept himself free from some portion of
political intemperance, some manifestation of party passion and
prejudice. On the other hand, personal feelings of hope or
disappointment, doubtless created for Governor McKean many
enemies. Yet during the whole constitutional period of nine
years, the majority of the people were with him; and at
the present day, when the party asperities and bickerings of

[1] Ibid., i., 526.
[2] Ibid., i., 527–9.
[3] Hildrith's *United States*, v., 666.

the times are in some measure forgotten, it cannot be denied that his administration was marked by uncommon ability, and with great benefit to the State.[1] Nevertheless, party asperities rose to such a height, that early in this year 1807, the federalists, led on by a few radicals, made an unsuccessful attempt to impeach Governor McKean. The charges were however chiefly allegations of political offenses;[2] and their frivolity and weakness may be seen by a perusal of them in the report of the committee to whom the matter was referred.

The proceedings commenced on the 30th of January, 1807, by Dr. Michael Leib, offering a resolution that a committee be appointed to inquire whether the official conduct of the Governor be such as to require the interposition of the House. This resolution, slightly modified, was adopted March 3d. In furtherance of this scheme, various petitions from citizens politically opposed to Governor McKean, were about this time presented to the house, and on the 2d of March the matter was referred to a committee consisting of Dr. Leib, Messrs. Lowry, Kerr, Lacock and Shewell. Mr. Huston was subsequently appointed in place of Mr. Lowry, who had received leave of absence. On Monday, the 30th of March, the committee submitted a report, containing the following charges, with specifications to each:

" I. That the governor did premeditatedly, wantonly, unjustly, and contrary to the true intent and meaning of the constitution, render void the late election, (in 1806,) of a sheriff in the county of Philadelphia.

" II. That he usurped a judicial authority, in issuing a warrant for the arrest and imprisonment of Joseph Cabrera; and interfered in favor of a convict for forgery, in defiance of the law, and contrary to the wholesome regulations of the prison in Philadelphia, and the safety of the citizens.

" III. That, contrary to the true intent and meaning of the constitution, and in violation of it, did he appoint Dr. George Buchanan, lazaretto physician of the port of Philadelphia.

" IV. That, under a precedent, acknowledged to have been derived from the king of Great Britain, and contrary to the express letter of the constitution, did he suffer his name to be stamped upon blank patents, warrants on the treasury, and other public official papers, and that too out of his presence.

" V. That, contrary to law, did he supersede Dr. James Reynolds, as a member of the board of health."

---

[1] Sanderson's *Lives.* Written about 1820.

[2] Armor's *Lives Govs. Penn.*

"VI. That, contrary to the obligation of duty, and the injunctions of the constitution, did he offer and authorize overtures to be made to discontinue two actions of the commonwealth against William Duane and his surety, for an alleged forfeiture of two recognizances of one thousand dollars each, on condition that William Duane would discontinue civil action against his son, Joseph B. McKean, and others, for a murderous assault committed by Joseph B. McKean and others on William Duane."

Accompanying the report was a resolution that Governor McKean be impeached for high crimes and misdemeanors. The report is partly quoted in Sanderson's Lives, in order to show its strong partisan character. It states that "the rights of the people of the city and county of Philadelphia have been grossly trifled with" by the Governor in rendering void the election for sheriff; that Dr. George Buchanan was appointed lazaretto physician while he was a resident of Baltimore; but for want of space we must forego further quotations.

On the report of the committee, the second reading was postponed until Thursday; nothing however appears in the journal on that day, but on Tuesday April 7, the motion for a second reading was debated, as also on the 8th and 9th, but could not be carried, and on the latter day the subject was postponed for the early consideration of the next house.[1]

In the fall of the year, says Scharf and Westcott, "the stubborn and aristocratic old Governor McKean, as soon as the legislature assembled, was greatly assailed by his enemies."[2] The impeachment resolution of the last house came up as unfinished business, December 7, six days after the legislature met. The next day Mr. John Sergeant seconded by Mr. Biddle (both members from Philadelphia,) moved to postpone the further consideration thereof until the second Monday in January, 1808; lost by a vote of 42 to 42. Mr. Lacock, seconded by Mr. Jennings, then moved to refer the matter to a select committee, which was lost by the same vote. On Friday, January 15th, 1808, Mr. Shewell seconded by Mr. Hulme, moved to consider the matter, but the motion was lost by a vote of 43 to 43. On Wednesday the 27th of January, Mr. Shewell seconded by Mr. Tarr, renewed his motion to consider the resoultion, which then prevailed by a vote of 44 to 41. It should be observed that these motions proceeded from the party friendly to Governor McKean, who were anxious to determine the validity of the charges.

---

[1] *Journals of the 17th H. R. of Penn.*, Lancaster, 1806.
[2] i., 532–3.

The resolution was now fairly before the house, and on motion of Mr. Porter, seconded by Mr. Shewell, the further consideration of the subject was indefinitely postponed by a vote of 44 to 41; which finally disposed of the whole matter.[1]

It may be added that every member from the city of Philadelphia, whose rights were said to be particularly infringed, voted for the governor, namely: Messrs. Sergeant, Clawges, Sr., Hare and Cope (subsequently elected in place of Samuel Carver, deceased before taking his seat).

On the next day, the 28th, the Secretary of the Commonwealth, Thomas McKean Thompson, appeared before the house, and presented a replication from the Governor, dated Lancaster, January 28, 1808, in relation to the charges against him. Mr. Sergeant, seconded by Mr. Ingham, moved that the message be inserted at large upon the journal; whereupon a spirited debate arose, but the motion finally prevailed by a vote of 43 to 42. Mr. Leib then moved that the report of the committee, with all the accompanying papers, be also inserted in the Journal, which was agreed to by a vote of 78 to 7.[2]

The papers upon both sides, here entered upon the Journal, are very voluminous. The testimony before the committee is given in full: Thomas McKean Thompson. Secretary of the Commonwealth, testified that the order making void the election of sheriff was not signed by the Governor, but was stamped in his presence; he was then unable to hold a pen in his hand; that he had been confined to his bed for five weeks, that he was at times in great pain, and unable to sit up in bed or to use his hands; but his mind was sound. That his name was stamped on public papers in his presence, but never out of it.

Dr. George Buchanan testified that he was a resident of Maryland until he arrived in Pennsylvania; and received his

---

[1] The following voted *aye* in favor of Governor McKean: George Acker, Paul Appel, William Barnet, Nathaniel Beach, Samuel Bethel, William S. Biddle, Valentine Brobst, John Clawges, Sr., Thomas P. Cope, Isaac Darlington, Jacob Eichelberger, Josiah Espy, George Evans, Robert Gemmill, James Gettys, Jacob Gisch (Gish), Charles W. Hare, John Hulme, Samuel D. Ingham (afterwards Secretary of Treasury under Pres. Jackson), Daniel Ioder (Joder), James Kelton, Bernard Kepner, Jacob Kimmell, John Lobingier, Benj. Martin, Robert Maxwell, John McClellan, James McComb, James McSherry, Charles Miner, William Pennock, Charles Porter, William Ramsey, Abraham Rinker, Daniel Rose, George Savitz, John Sergeant, Jacob Shaeffer, Conrad Sherman, Nathaniel Shewell, Charles Smith (Lancaster Co.), William Trimble, William Worthington, John Wright—44.

[2] *Journals* 18*th H. R. Penn.*, Lancaster, 1807. See also Sanderson's *Lives.*

commission as Lazaretto Physician the day after he arrived ; that he was a candidate for Congress from Maryland in 1803-4.
The Governor's physicians testified that they were first called to attend the Governor January 20th, that he had some fever, and a gouty affection, but no delirium.[1]

The Replication of the Governor commences as follows :

" A long and dangerous illness, the sympathy of friends, and the advice of physicians, deprived me of an opportunity to peruse the journal, or to have the least knowledge of the proceedings in relation to an impeachment of my official conduct, for more than a month after the termination of the last session of the General Assembly.   And since that period, a proper respect for the exercise of constitutional powers has restrained every disposition on my part, to answer the charges which have been exhibited against me, while those charges continued a subject of deliberation.   But the delicacy which has recognized your constitutional jurisdiction, must not be allowed to absorb every consideration that is due to my own fame, to the feelings of my family, and to the opinion of the world.

" The accusation, though not confirmed by the ultimate vote of the house, has been deliberately framed, has been openly discussed, and will pass among the legislative records, into the hands of our constituents, and our posterity, with all its concomitant semblance of proof, and asperity of animadversion.   The decision that expresses your renunciation of the impeachment, affects me indeed, with its justice and its independence ; but it is a decision which precludes the employment of the regular means of defence before a proper tribunal ; and therefore compels me, for the purpose of vindication, to claim a page in the same volume, that serves to perpetuate against me, the imputation of official crimes and misdemeanors.

" It is incompatible, gentlemen, with my view of the solemnity of the occasion, to descend to the language of invective or complaint.   By exposing the depravity of other men, I should do little to demonstrate my own innocence ; and an expression of sensibility at any personal indignity that has been inflicted, might be construed into an encroachment upon the freedom of legislative debate.   But the tenor of my public and private life, will I hope be sufficient to repel every vague and declamatory aspersion. The discernment of our constituents will readily detect any latent motive of hatred and malice.   The justice of the Legislature upholds an ample shield against the spirit of persecution ; and the conscious rectitude of my own mind will yield a lasting consolation, amidst all the vicissitudes of popular favor and applause.* *

---

[1] *Journals*, etc.

"That I may have erred in judgment, that I may have been mistaken in my general views of public policy, and that I may have been deceived by the objects of executive confidence, or benevolence, I am not so vain nor so credulous as to deny; though in the present instance, I am still without the proof and without the belief: but the firm and fearless position which I take, invites the strictest scrutiny, upon a fair exposition of our constitution and laws, into the sincerity and truth of the general answer given to my accusers, *that no act of my public life was ever done from a corrupt motive ; nor without a deliberate opinion that the act was lawful and proper in itself.*"[1]

Governor McKean then proceeds in a circumstantial and irrefutable manner, separately to repel the charges of the committee ; and triumphantly to vindicate his character in every particular, from the aspersions with which it had been assailed.

His refutation of the charges is briefly as follows :

I. The election for sheriff was made void under the act of the Assembly of February 15, 1790, "That the Governor shall be a competent judge of the election of every person who shall be returned to serve as sheriff or coroner ; and for that purpose may send for papers, persons or records." The investigation was intrusted to a committee of seven persons, of whom Joseph Reed was chairman. The committee examined witnesses and reported a list of " 96 bad votes " cast, which they threw out for various reasons ;—illegal voting, not of age, not naturalized, voted in the wrong precinct, etc. If this number should be deducted from Wolbert who had 3905 votes, then Lawler who had 3846 would have been elected. It could not be ascertained for whom the votes were cast. Hence the doubt who was elected, and the Governor issued a proclamation to this effect, declaring the election void, and that the present sheriff holds over until the next election.

Wolbert, accompained by General Barker, called upon the Governor to obtain his commission. The Governor refused to see them ; and states in his replication, as follows : " It has also been developed upon the oath of General Barker, that an attempt was then to be made to obtain a commission for Mr. Wolbert, by offers of favor, or menaces of vengeance ; by giving the Governor the option of 'the sword or the olive branch;' and by a denunciation, (which General Barker swears came from the tongue of Dr. Michael Leib the chair-

---

[1] As quoted in Sanderson's *Lives.*

man of the committee of impeachment, and similar menaces of assassination were contained in anonymous letters received through the post-office,) 'that if the old scoundrel, or old rascal, did not acceed to the proposal, he would pursue him to the grave.'"

II. Joseph Cabrera was imprisoned upon the request of the Spanish Minister. The minister has a right to imprison a member of the legation in his own domicile, and has power to send him home for trial. He also has an unquestionable claim upon the government to guard his prisoner; this is then regarded not as judicial, but an executive recognizance. Moreover, at the trial, Cabrera waived his diplomatic privileges. As to the second part of the charge, after his conviction, the Governor says a power to grant pardon and reprieve of the whole sentence, naturally includes the power to pardon any part of it; and this was done also at the request of the minister.

III. Dr. Buchanan's appointment. Under the constitution certain offices must be filled by residents of the county in which the office is located; but this does not apply to the office of Secretary of the Commonwealth, Secretary, Receiver General, etc., because then all the counties in the state would not have equal rights. The Lazaretto Physician is not a county officer, but an officer of the port of Philadelphia, his office being a department of the board of health, and since the office was created, there is no instance of a resident of the county in which it is located, having filled it. Dr. Buchanan is not an alien, but a citizen of the United States.

IV. The law requires the Governor to *sign*, but does not specify the kind of signature. A cross is a valid signature, and in case of the loss of both hands it is hard to imagine how a person could sign, if restructed to writing his name. He also adds, "Although the Governor did not always affix the signature to official papers with his own hand, it was never affixed without his express order."

V. Dr. Reynolds was removed for intemperance and violence; he struck a member of the board of health, which act was complained of to the Governor, who counselled a delay; but on the offense being repeated, the other members of the board resigned, whereupon the Governor at once removed Dr. Reynolds. The act of the legislature, directs that members of the board of health should hold office for one year; but this was not meant to enlarge the tenure but to limit it, for the legislature provided for cases of death, sickness, removal, etc., which implies power of the Governor to remove.

VI. This charge is based upon overtures made by Messrs. Ingersoll, Dallas, Muhlenberg, and Dickerson, but they have expressly declared in writing, that they were unauthorized by the Governor to make overtures. The Governor states the facts of the quarrel briefly as follows: The troops of light horse was engaged in suppressing a disturbance in Berks and Northampton counties ; and the *Aurora* charged that they " lived at free quarters." The officers called for a retraction, an altercation ensued, and they chastised the editor.[1]

Thus did Governor McKean refute the charges made against him. He had however to contend, not only against the ostensible charges, but also against the vindictiveness and malignancy of the radical members of the committee. The charge that the Governor imprisoned Cabrera, and then allowed him privileges after conviction ;— that is, complaining of what the Governor did *against* him, as well as what he did *in his favor*, savors more of opposition to the Governor than solicitude for Cabrera's welfare. The animus of the mover of these proceedings, Dr. Leib, is shown in the testimony of John Barker before the committee, Dr. Leib being present:

" The Dr. [Leib] then arrested my attention by calling me general, and told me to remember, general, we offer him the sword or the olive branch, let him take his choice. I did not consider this to be secrets. I looked upon myself as a kind of ambassador. After the Dr. gave me this last instruction, he exclaimed with some warmth, That if the old scoundrel or old rascal did not accede to these proposals, he would pursue him to the grave."[2]

To the Sixth Charge, it is related in Hildrith's History, that Governor McKean retorted by having Leib, Duane, and others indicted for conspiracy to corrupt and overawe him.[3]

Governor McKean's replication comprehends a very learned and masterly disquisition; defining in a most lucid manner the powers and duties of the several branches of the government, legislative, judicial and executive ; and expounding clearly impeachable offences. And upon repeated references to it, it has been found to bear the cautious scrutiny of unimpassioned judgment, and to furnish a clear, safe, and useful

[1]*Journals* 18th *H. R. Penn.*
[2]*Journals* 18th *H. R. Penn.*, 1807, p. 349.
[3]*Hist. U. S.*. vi., 67.

guide in the elucidation of cases involving points similar to those which he professes to discuss. It is regarded with great favor by professional men, and is quoted as authority upon the questions of which it treats.[1] Thus terminated a transaction, which through the baleful and exterminating spirit of party, threatened to overshadow the closing career of a patriot, whose life, during half a century, had been devoted to the public service.[2]

CLOSE OF HIS TERM OF OFFICE—RETIRES TO PRIVATE LIFE.

Governor McKean had now served as the executive of Pennsylvania for nine years, through three terms of office; his services must necessarily be brought to a close by constitutional limitation. The impeachment proceedings, the strongest card played by his enemies, having signally failed, further asperities were suspended; and in the following fall, Simon Snyder was nominated against Ross, Governor McKean's first competitor. Snyder was elected, and assumed the executive chair December 20, 1808. The same party was yet in power; and Leib and Duane, leaders of the same faction, still kept up their abuse. After the campaign closed, Duane of the *Aurora* was again pelted with lawsuits; John Binns one of this faction published an article in which he said "under McKean the legislature was bullied and abused; under Snyder it was caucussed and corrupted."[3] It is here gratifying to find in the writings of his enemies, that which redounds to his credit; he may have " bullied " or " abused," but he never "corrupted " the legislature. This statement and the inference to be drawn from it comes opportunely, not long after Governor McKean's statement in his Replication; that no act of his public life was ever done from a *corrupt* motive.

At the end of his term of office, Governor McKean retired to private life, having been before the public continuously, and in many of the highest offices for forty-six years. He was at the time of his retirement nearly seventy-five years of age; but his vigor was not diminished by his years.

"For nine successive years," says a contemporary,[4] "he

[1] W. H. Egle, *Hist. Penn.*, i., 235; and Sanderson's *Lives*.

[2] Sanderson's *Lives*.

[3] Scharf and Westcott, i., 533–45. See Duane's obituary on a subsequent page.

[4] L. Carroll Judson, of the Philadelphia bar, *Biog. of Signers*, 1839.

wielded the destines of the land of Pennsylvania, commencing at a period when the mountain waves of party spirit were rolling over the United States, with a fury before unknown. But amid the foaming and conflicting elements, Governor McKean stood at the helm of state, calm as a summer morning, firm as a mountain of granite, and guided his noble ship through the raging storm, unscathed and unharmed. His annual messages to the legislature, for elegance and force of language, correct and liberal views of policy, and a luminous exposition of law and rules of government, stand unrivalled, and unsurpassed. The clamour of his political enemies, he passed by as the idle wind; the suggestions of his friends, he scanned with the most rigid scrutiny. Neither flattery nor censure could drive him from the strong citadel of his own matured judgment. The good of his country, and the glory of the American character, formed the grand basis of his actions.

"His administration was prosperous and enlightened, and when he closed his political duties, the bitterness of his political opponents was lost in the admiration of his patriotism, virtue, impartiality, consistency, and candor."

Says another writer:

Perhaps no man attracted so much homage from the crowd as Governor McKean, not only as Delegate in Congress, and Chief Justice, but especially in his old age. He was one of that old stock of Pennsylvanians, of abnormal size and strength in both mind and body. He was tall and stately—over six feet in height; and even in later years, notwithstanding his great age, an erect person. He usually wore a cocked hat, carried a gold-headed cane; and walked, even to the close of his life, though with a somewhat tottered step, with great apparent dignity and pride. As is known, he was one of the Signers of the Declaration of Independence, and if we may use the phrase, which we do in all respect and kindness, he was an actual impersonification—a practical living, walking emblem, and memento, of that Declaration. Apparently the two proudest men the city ever beheld—and sure they had much to be proud of—were our present venerable subject, and his son-in-law, the Marquis de Casa Yrujo, the ambassador from Spain.[1]

FEARS OF A BRITISH INVASION—PRESIDES AT A TOWN MEETING, 1814.

During the last war with England, Philadelphia was startled by the news that a British army was on our shores. The city was wholly unprepared for any defence; and a number of the

---

[1] David Paul Brown, *The Forum*, i., 346. See also *Harp. Mag.*, lii., 871.

most influential citizens met and at once issued a call for a town-meeting on the morning of August 26th. Washington had been captured the day before, but the fact was not known at that time. The meeting convened in the State House square. Ex-Governor McKean had been particularly desired to attend, and on his appearing once more among his countrymen on a public occasion, he was greeted with profound respect and attention ; and was unanimously called to take the chair. He was at this time eighty years of age. Joseph Reed, another patriot of the revolution, was made secretary. Never since the revolutionary period, had a public meeting been held in Philadelphia on so momentous a business ; and never since the same period, had an occasion existed, which demanded more promptness and decision of action. No noisy demagogues attempted to control its operations, or to create excitement by inflammatory harangues. The venerable chairman alone addressed it, and in a few brief sentences, delivered with the dignity and emphasis of former days, touched the spirit that needed only to be awakened. His speech made a deep impression, and was recognized as coming from a patriot and a sage. The meeting, without waste of time, and without useless discussion, took the measures which the crisis demanded ; and the city was in a short time placed in a condition to repel the attack of any force which the enemy could then bring against it.[1]

The "Committee of Defense, 1814," appointed by this meeting, consisted of the officers of the meeting, prominent movers, and a number of other citizens.[2]

HONORARY DEGREES, DIPLOMAS, HONORS, ETC.

Governor McKean received the honorary degree of A. M. from the University of Pennsylvania, in 1763 ; and LL. D. from the College of New Jersey, in 1781, September 26 ; and from Dartmouth College, New Hampshire, in 1782 ; and from the University of Pennsylvania, in 1785. He was a Trustee of the University of Pennsylvania, in 1779, under the University Charter ; and in 1791, November 18th, at the Union.[3]

---

[1] Sanderson's *Lives ;* see also *National Portraits,* vol. for 1839 ; and Scharf and Westcott, i., 571.

[2] The names may be found in Scharf and Westcott, *Hist.,* iii., 1769 ; and in John Hill Martin's *Bench and Bar of Phila.* The Minutes of the Committee of Defence were published in the Memoirs of the Historical Society of Pennsylvania, 1867, vol. 8.

[3] College Catalogues, Univ. Penn. Catalogue, 1880.

Governor McKean was elected a member of the Philadelphia Society for the Promotion of Agriculture, May 2d, 1785.[1] It was instituted February 11, 1785.

October 31, 1785, he received his diploma of the Society of the Cincinnati, instituted by officers of the American Army, at the close of the Revolution.[2] He subsequently became Vice-President of the Pennsylvania State Society. The author has been unsuccessful in finding any lists of the Pennsylvania Society, containing Governor McKean's name. In the Department of State at Washington however, is a letter of Thomas McKean and others, dated Philadelphia, March 6, 1787, addressed to General Washington, in reply to his circular letter of October 31st, declining to be re-elected to the presidency; this letter concludes by expressing regret at General Washington's determination; and states that his request will be laid before the meeting of the state society, called for the 26th instant, and will be intimated to the delegates to the general triennial meeting; it is signed by a committee of the Society, Thomas McKean, W. Jackson, and F. Mentger.

In 1770 or earlier, Thomas McKean, of Newcastle, was elected a member of the American Philosophical Society. In 1786 or earlier, while Chief Justice, he became one of the twelve Councillors; and in 1799 as Governor he became ex-officio the Patron of the Society.[3]

In 1790, while Chief Justice, he was one of the founders of the Hibernian Society for the relief of emigrants from Ireland, and the first president.

In 1804, McKean county was separated from Lycoming county, Pennsylvania, and named in honor of Thomas McKean, at that time Governor.[4]

McKean street, in Philadelphia, is also named after him.

In 1786, was published "*The Lyric Works of Horace*" by John Parke, with an appendix containing poems by John Wilcocks, and dedicated to General Washington. The several poems being addressed to the prominent men of the day; Ode V, Book III, as also the Secular Poem, *Carmen Seculare*, are both addressed to Thomas McKean then Chief Justice, Vice President of the Cincinnati, and late President of Con-

[1] Sanderson's *Lives.*
[2] Sanderson, *The Forum*, etc.
[3] *Transactions.*
[4] Egle's *Hist Penn.;* Day's *Histor. Collect.*

8-*b*

gress. An Elegy on the death of Colonel John Haselet of
Delaware is addressed to Cæsar Rodney and Thomas McKean,
members of Congress.

HIS DEATH AND FUNERAL.

At length, loaded with honors, this venerable patriot arrived
at the *ultima linea rerum*, and departed to "the generation
of his fathers" on the 24th of June, 1817, aged eighty-three
years, two months and twenty-five days.[1]
    In the *United States Gazette* of the following day, ap-
peared the notice :

"Another Patriot of '76 descended to the Tomb.
    Died yesterday, the 24th inst., Thomas McKean, Esq., formerly
Governor of Pennsylvania.
    " The gentlemen of the bar are requested to attend the funeral
of the late *Thomas McKean, Esq.*, formerly governor of Pennsylvania, from his late mansion, south Third street to-morrow
morning at 9 o'clock.
    " The Members of the Society of the Cincinnati are requested
to attend the funeral of the late *Thomas McKean, Esq.*, formerly
governor of Pennsylvania, from his late mansion, south Third
street to-morrow morning at 9 o'clock.
    "The Members of the Hibernian Society are requested to at-
tend the funeral of the late *Thomas McKean, Esq.*, formerly governor of Pennsylvania, from his late mansion, south Third street
to-morrow morning at 9 o'clock.
    "The Members of the Philosophical Society are requested to
attend the funeral of the late *Thomas McKean, Esq.*, formerly
governor of Pennsylvania, from his late mansion, south Third
street to-morrow morning at 9 o'clock.
    " The Trustees of the University of Pennsylvania are re-
quested to attend the funeral of the late *Thomas McKean, Esq.*,
formerly governor of Pennsylvania, from his late mansion, south
Third street to-morrow morning at 9 o'clock."   -

In this paper of Thursday the 26th, appeared a set of Resolutions of respect, passed by the Philadelphia Bar.
    In *Poulsen's American Daily Advertiser* of the 25th ap-
peared a short notice of his death "between the hours of two

---

[1] Not 16 days, as given in Sanderson's *Lives*. Every succeeding biographer has copied this mistake. Not one has thought of verifying it. The
difference between the dates of birth and death gives 83 years, 3 months, 5
days; but his birth being given in *old style*, eleven days must be deducted,
and (adding 31 days for May, the previous month to that of his death, to
make the subtraction possible,) we have his age as given above.

and three o'clock;" followed the next day, by a long obituary and notice of his death similar to that given above.

On the 27th appeared a long editorial notice commencing as follows:

"GOVERNOR McKEAN. The late THOMAS McKEAN, formerly Chief Justice and afterwards Governor of Pennsylvania; of whose political conduct, however varied may be the judgment of the different Parties which divide the State, there can be but one opinion as to his regard for the public weal, in his successive nominations of eminent characters of different political sentiments, to succeed him in the judicial chair; an instance of patriotic impartiality so rare in public life that it must be allowed on all hands to reflect peculiar honor on his memory. * * * *"

In the *General Advertiser* of June 25th, *The Aurora*, and still published by Governor McKean's old political opponent, William Duane, pays the following noble tribute to his memory:

"DIED—yesterday at three o'clock, Thomas McKean, LL.D. one of the earliest and most firm friends of American independence; some time a representative in the Continental Congress, of which he was also president; many years Chief Justice of this commonwealth; and closed[1] his long and eventful career by serving as Governor for nine years in this commonwealth. Mr. McKean was a native of this state, of an old Irish stock, and derived from his progenitors a considerable share of energy and decision of character; in the most trying times, of the revolution, he was among those who never wavered, and who spurned the royal favor offered to him, preferring to such honors, and venal rewards, the prouder honors of devotion to his country and liberty. It is to his name due, that it should be remembered, that although of an energy not to be resisted in a public station, that by his kindness of heart many who had mistaken the path of true honor in forsaking their country to serve a tyrant were by his private generosity rescued from public vengeance, and the inexorable law. As a judge it must be acknowledged that he gave the laws dignity by enforcing them; his rigor obtained for him many enemies; but time, which has drawn the thorn of individual resentment, will do justice to the austerity which was directed as much as human passions can admit, to equal and exact justice. In the station of governor he incurred the same censure; and it must be confessed deservedly: but the experience of the administration which succeeded his has interposed a relief, which by comparison reduces the exceptionable parts of Mr. McKean's administration to the small sins of passion or pride. He was much better adapted to the bench of justice, than the executive chair. In the former

---

[1] So given ungrammatically.

he displayed the severity of Cethegus, and the probity of Cato ; his principles were strictly republican, but he held that education should be the first care of a free people, because there is no danger so much to be apprehended as ignorance. If he did not always direct his energy against ignorance, in the proper time and manner, it was the effect, rather of constitutional warmth than any worse passion, as no man more sincerely deplored such aberrations than himself. He was in short a man devoted to whatever he conceived to be just—a most faithful citizen, and earnest friend of his country, and its liberty, and independence."

In the *Gentleman's Magazine*, London 1817, appears a short notice of Governor McKean's death.

His remains were interred in the burial ground of the First Presbyterian Church in Market street, Philadelphia ; the only record among the church archives being in the book of interments kept by an illiterate sexton: " 1817, June 26, thomas McKean."

Subsequently the remains were removed to the family vault of his grandson, Henry Pratt McKean, Esq., in Laurel Hill Cemetery, Philadelphia, over which, on a large plain altar tomb,[1] is the following inscription :

McKEAN FAMILY VAULT.

Beneath
this marble
are
the remains
of THOMAS McKEAN,
one of the Signers
of the
Declaration of Independence,
President of Congress in 1781,
Chief Justice
and
Governor
of the
State of Pennsylvania,
Born, March 19, 1734,
died, June 24, 1817.
And the DESCENDANTS of his
FAMILY.

---

[1] Mentioned in *The Official Guide Book of Phila.*, Thompson Westcott, 1875.

HIS LIFE AND CHARACTER.

The reader who has perused this biography will, I doubt not, have already formed his own estimate of Thomas McKean's character. In the many extracts already given, from the writings of judges, lawyers and historians,—his contemporaries and others,—his friends and opponents, there is no conflict of opinion upon this subject; and the general impression left on the mind of the reader, will convey a far more accurate estimate of Thomas McKean's character, than any brief summation in a single paragraph.

The great age attained by many of the Signers of the Declaration, and the exceedingly high average of their lives collectively, has been noted by historians;[1] four lived to be over 90, and eight others between 80 and 90. Of McKean, one of his biographers remarks that "For a man of so varied and such great labors, his length of life was remarkable, and illustrates the maxim, that sloth, like rust consumes faster than labor wears."[2]

At the close of Governor McKean's life there were living besides himself, five signers; these last survivors of that immortal group of patriots were as follows:[3]

Thomas McKean, born 1734, died 1817, aged 83 years 3 mo.
William Ellery, 1727 1820 92 2
William Floyd, 1734 1821 86 8
John Adams, 1735 1826 90 9
Thomas Jefferson, 1743 1826 83 2
Charles Carroll, 1737 1832 95 2

During his latter years Thomas McKean kept up a correspondence with Jefferson, Adams, and other revolutionary patriots. On hearing of his death, Mr. Adams immediately addressed the following letter, dated Quincy, June 30, 1817, to the editor of *Niles' Register*, as a tribute to his deceased friend:

"MR. NILES. The oldest statesman in North America is no more. Vixit. McKean, for whose services, and indeed for whose patronage the two states of Pennsylvania and Delaware once contended, is numbered with the fathers. I cannot express my feelings upon this event in any way, better, than by the publication

---

[1] *Goodrich*, preface.
[2] Armor.
[3] Lanman, *Biog. Annals*.

of the enclosed letters. [Here follow the dates of eight letters, the latest being June 17, 1817.] I pray you to print these letters in your Register.   JOHN ADAMS."

This letter and the enclosures, were accordingly published as requested on the 12th of July, (vol. xii, p. 305, *et seq*).

Mr. Adams on the 30th of December following, in a letter to John M. Jackson, speaks in the following high terms of Governor McKean:

"In 1774, I became acquainted with McKean, Rodney and Henry. [Patrick Henry.] Those three appeared to me to see more clearly to the end of the business than any others of the whole body. At least they were more candid and explicite with me than any others. Mr. Henry was in Congress in 1774, and a small part of 1775. He was called home by his state to take a military command. McKean and Rodney continued members, and, I believe I never voted in opposition to them in any one instance."[1]

It will undoubtedly have been noticed in this biography, that Thomas McKean was an eminently successful man in life, and essentially a leader among men. Moreover he had the true training of a leader,—that of beginning in a lower station and ascending. So marked is this, that when the colonies were arming themselves in 1775, Mr. McKean, although filling the exalted station of a delegate in congress, hesitated not to enroll himself in the army as a *private*. As a lawyer he soon took a leading stand in his profession; as a member of the Assembly he rose to be Speaker; in congress he became President; as a judge he rose from the lower courts to the highest judicial office, that of Chief Justice; in the army from being a private, he became colonel, his province however lay not in military, but in civil life. As Governor, he filled the highest office in the state. In numerous committees, conventions and public meetings, he either directed their proceedings as chairman, or else was a leading spirit on the floor. In no case do we find him receding; even during the stormy days while in the gubernatorial chair of Pennsylvania; and in no case do we find him stationary in any line until he has reached the highest rank therein.

I cannot better close this biography, than with the concluding paragraph in Sanderson's Lives:

Thomas McKean outlived all the enmities[2] which an active

---

[1] *Works*, x., 269.

[2] After a perusal of everything that I can find, in print, regarding Thomas

and conspicuous part in public affairs, had in the nature of things, created ; and posterity will continue to cherish his memory, as one among the most useful, able, and virtuous fathers of a mighty republic.

Conscia mens recti, famæ mendacia ridet.

HIS WILL AND SEAL THERETO.

Thomas McKean's will is a holograph will, made, as he himself says, when he has passed his eightieth year. It covers seven pages of large sized unruled paper, and is dated very appropriately August 13, 1814, "and of the independence of the United States of America, the thirty-ninth." He firsts directs "that my funeral may be decent but not expensive." To his wife, he leaves the choice of his household furniture to the value of $1000; and $600 per annum, and also a house in Holmesburgh. Forty thousand dollars advanced to his children is remitted and released to them.

To Joseph B. McKean, his mansion house in Philadelphia, the pictures in the hall of the house, gold-headed cane, "my steel-seal ring with my coat of Arms cut thereon," Family bible, Notes of cases, and all his manuscripts.

To Mary McKean only child of his son Robert, deceased, a house in Holmesburgh.

To Andrew Pettit for the four sons and four daughters of his deceased daughter Elizabeth, 11 tracts of land on Brush creek Beaver co., 2200 acres, and also some rent charges.

To Lætitia Buchanan, land on the Ohio river Beaver co. near Logstown, six tracts, 1580 acres ; also a plantation called Pottersfield in the new county of Centre, 407 acres worth $40 per acre.

To the four children of Anne Buchanan, (to Joseph B. McKean in trust,) tracts of land on the N. W. of the Ohio river, 1116 acres ; and a tract of 404 acres in Haines's township, Luzerne co. and some rent charges.

To his daughter Sarah Maria Theresa, Marchioness de Casa Yrujo, 8 tracts on the Sewickly creek, Allegheny co., 2266 acres 52 perches.

McKean, (and the references here given will show that this search has not been limited,) I am happy to testify that this statement is *true*. William Duane, his most violent opponent, pays him a generous tribute in his obituary ; and among recent writers, I have found but two who have written against him, namely, William T. Read, in 1870 : and a historical writer in the Village Record of West Chester, Pa., 1860, both quoted in these pages.

To Thomas McKean, plantation called Chatham, 392 acres
in London Grove township, Chester co. and 6 acres of chestnut
wood six miles distant, also "my silver-hilted small sword, my
stock, knee and shoe buckles," and his folio hot press bible.
To his daughter Sophia Dorothea, 4 tracts in Centre co.,
1684 acres 32 perches ; two lots on Spruce street between
Sixth and Seventh streets.
To his grandson Samuel M. McKean, plantation in Mt.
Equity 300 acres, in McKean co.
His executors may sell 5 acres on Logan street Phila. co.;
and about 440 acres, and a tract of 150 acres in Newcastle,
Del.

"All the rest of my estate, real and personal, I give devise,
and bequeathe to my grandchildren Thomas McKean Pettit,
McKean Buchanan, Thomas McKean Buchanan, Charles Ferdi-
nand de Yrujo, and Henry Pratt McKean, and their heirs and
assigns forever, as tenants in common."

Joseph B. McKean, Andrew Pettit, and Thomas McKean
are named as executors.
Witnessed by Jared Ingersoll and Jos: Reed ; Proved June
27, 1817, and recorded in Philadelphia, No. 90, lib. 6, fol.
467.
The will is sealed with red sealing-wax, about the size of a
quarter of a dollar, now somewhat broken on one side ; but
enough remains to show the impression of a coat of arms, sub-
stantially the same as those on David Edwin's engraving of
Stuart's painting.

COAT OF ARMS.

There is no coat of arms in this family that I believe to be
genuine. The arms under David Edwin's engraving, and the
same as used by Governor McKean on the seal of his will, are
as follows :

ARMS : *Or, four pallets gules, debruised by a bend sinister azure,
charged with a crescent decrescent argent, between two mullets of
six points, of the same.*
CREST : *An eagle crested, with wings displayed, perched upon a
snake, with head erected.*
MOTTO : *Mens sana in corpore sano.*

In a copy of *McKean's Laws* at the Library of the Supreme Court of the United States, there is a book plate of
these arms, (the only book plate of them I have seen or heard

of,) with the tinctures clearly shown; and identical with the above, save that the divisions of the shield are *paly of eight*, instead of nine. Below the arms on a drapery is the name McKean, in script letters, and below that the engraver's name, *M. de Bruls.*

These arms, I believe to be spurious; but when or by whom first assumed I know not. My chief reasons are as follows: 1st. No McKean family in England carries such arms; of the three families named in *Burke's General Armory*, two carry a saltire, and the other three trefoils. 2d. No one would voluntarily carry the bend sinister. 3d. There is two great a similarity to the "stars and stripes" in the shield,—to the American eagle in the crest,—and the motto is a household word. 4. Judge Thomas McKean Pettit, with a patriotic notion discarded his proper crest, and substituted therefore an eagle almost identical to that in the above arms, save that in these, the eagle is *crested*, and in the Pettit, *not crested, re-guardant*. And what is more likely than this having been done by Judge Pettit, in imitation of his grandsire?

In some branches of the family, these arms are well known, through David Edwin's engraving, and from colored drawings; but none of Judge Joseph B. McKean's descendants know anything of the "steel seal ring" willed by Governor McKean to his eldest son, and from which I had hoped to gain some information about these arms.

Our relative Henry Pettit Esq., of Philadelphia, who is interested in family history, and has made some researches as to a coat of arms, writes under date of February 26, 1886: "If the McKeans ever had any crest or arms, I should like greatly to see it, never having come across it as yet." In reply I mentioned these spurious arms; and not long after received a letter dated June 17, 1886, containing the following interesting extract:

"In a previous letter you wrote with regard to the often asked for McKean arms. I think myself, that there really are none. I have never seen the so-called arms you refer to, but if ever you come across anything engraved or photoed, or representing the so-called McKean arms, I should like, from curiosity to see it. One reason is this,—About the beginning of this century there seems to have been quite a craze, to get up in some families, an *American modification* of the English Arms the families had previously worn; and the result was remarkable, from a herald's point of view in many cases. I had myself a book plate of the Pettit arms so changed, with eagle for crest, and helmet, vizor up

full faced, which had been *purposely changed* by Judge Thomas
McKean Pettit, from his grandfather Charles Pettit's arms, in
order to *Americanize it*, and get rid purposely of all the English
except the arms proper; and by the eagle show the American
branch. I showed these arms as a joke at the College of Arms,
London, and I thought the Herald would have split with laughter.
Nevertheless it showed the *American independent spirit rampant*
at that period. Now I am disposed to think that a McKean
plate, arms, crest, and motto, all complete, was devised by some
patriotic McKeanite, say about that same time, eagle as usual,
and all other American features."

PORTRAITS, HISTORICAL PAINTINGS AND ENGRAVINGS OF GOVERNOR McKEAN.

1. AN OIL PORTRAIT BY GILBERT STUART, and considered
one of his masterpieces, on a panel formerly in possession of
the eldest son, Joseph B. McKean, now in possession of the
latter's grandson Samuel M. McKean. It is a half length,
showing the left side, and the badge of the Cincinnati on the
left breast, the head turned nearly full face. In the *Life and
Works of Gilbert Stuart* by George C. Mason, N. Y., 1879,
this picture is catalogued with the encomium, "An upright
Chief Justice, an enlightened lawyer, a sagacious politician, he
was looked up to as one of the most reliable men of the day."
*By this portrait Governor McKean is best known to pos-
terity, several engravings having been made from it.*

2. OIL PORTRAIT; Copy of the previous, by Marchant,
owned by the Law Association of Philadelphia; and which
has been loaned to the Supreme Court since 1875; it hangs
in the place of honor behind the Judge's Bench on the right
side.[1]

3. OIL PORTRAIT; Copy of Stuart (No. 1,) by James R.
Lambdin, and presented by him to the Pennsylvania Historical
Society, Philadelphia, November 17, 1852. Numbered 141,
on the Society's Catalogue of Paintings.

4. IN THE OLD STATE HOUSE, *Independence Hall*, oil portrait by Peale. The *right* side of the face is shown.[2]

5. SIGNING THE DECLARATION OF INDEPENDENCE, by Trumbull. The original, 30x20 inches, is in the Trumbull Gallery
of Yale College. A copy made by the same artist, painted by

---

[1] See John Hill Martin, *Bench and Bar*, p. 222.

[2] See *Catalogue of Ind. Hall* for use of visitors, portrait numbered 11; also
Belisle's *Hist. Ind. Hall*, 1859; and F. M. Etting, *Histor. Acct. of Old State
Ho.*, 1876.

order of Congress, is one of the eight large historical paintings in the rotunda of the Capitol at Washington. Thomas McKean is one of the delegates here represented, and numbered 46. Not all the members of Congress are however included. The picture is well-known by engravings.[1]

6. WASHINGTON RESIGNING HIS COMMISSION, by Edwin White 1859, a large historical painting in the State House, Annapolis, Md. Thomas McKean is here represented among the delegates, and numbered 18 in the key engraving. As a matter of fact however the resignation took place December 23, 1783, and Mr. McKean's term had expired some months before ;—an anachronism, undoubtedly due to Mr. McKean's prominence and long service in Congress. Thomas Mifflin, president of Congress, Charles Carroll, Thomas Jefferson, and Edward Lloyd are also among the delegates shown. This is quite a different picture from that of Trumbull, representing the same scene, and which is another of the eight large paintings in the rotunda of the national Capitol.

7. LADY WASHINGTON'S RECEPTION DAY; by Daniel Huntington of New York. Thomas McKean is numbered 35, and is described in the key engraving as Chief · Justice of Pennsylvania. There are sixty-four likenesses in all. The artist very kindly informs me that the picture is 6x9 feet; and that it was painted in 1859-60, for A. H. Ritchie, the well-known engraver; who paid $2500 for it, and who made the steel engraving by which it is well known. This picture was recently in the collection of A. T. Stewart of New York, and was purchased at the sale of his pictures by the Hamilton Club of Brooklyn, for $3300. The likeness of Thomas McKean was painted from the engraving of Welch after Stuart.[2]

8. THE FIRST PRAYER IN CONGRESS ; September 1774. Painted by T. H. Matterson for the Carpenters' Company of Philadelphia, to commemorate the meeting of the first Congress in Carpenter's Hall. This picture is also well known from the engraving on steel by H. S. Sadd " From the original picture, painted expressly for this engraving," 1848. Thirty-three persons are represented. General Washington, No. 9, kneels in the foreground; Thomas McKean, No. 21, also kneels ; in the background stands Stephen Hopkins, No. 18, the Quaker from Rhode Island, with his hat on.

---

[1] See a paper by Lyman C. Draper; *Collections, State Hist. Soc. of Wis.*, vol. x.

[2] Letter of the Artist, June 19, 1888.

9. OIL PORTRAIT BY STUART, in possession of His Excellency the Marquis de Casa Yrujo, Madrid, Spain.

10. OIL PORTRAIT, Copy of Stuart's (No. 1) by McMurtrie of Philadelphia, made for Samuel M. McKean of Washington, and now in possession of his daughters.

11. OIL PORTRAIT BY CHARLES WILSON PEALE, in possession of Henry Pratt McKean Esq. of Philadelphia, a large painting with the Governor's son Thomas, at the age of about ten years, standing by his side.

12. OIL PORTRAIT BY CHARLES WILSON PEALE, presented to his daughter Elizabeth, on her marriage with Andrew Pettit, now in possession of Mrs. Sarah P. Wilson of Philadelphia.

13. OIL PORTRAIT; Artist unknown, on a panel, (It resembles Stuart's No. 1, and may be a copy ; the badge of the Cincinnati being shown). Formerly in possession of the Governor's daughter Lætitia Buchanan, and at her death passed to her son the late Admiral Franklin Buchanan. Now at his late residence, " The Rest," Talbot Co., Maryland.

There may be other portraits or copies that I have not heard of.

Engravings ; on steel or copper.

i. ENGRAVING by David Edwin, entitled " Thomas McKean, Governor of the Commonwealth of Pennsylvania, Vice President of the State Society of Cincinnati, etc." " Engraved by David Edwin, from the original Picture by Gilbert Stuart in the Possession of J. B. McKean Esq." It is about one-fourth of life size. I only know of five of these engravings, which are usually framed; doubtless there are many more. 1. In the author's possession. 2. Mrs. Admiral Buchanan, " The Rest," Maryland ; 3. The Misses Coale, Baltimore ; 4. Family of the late Samuel M. McKean of Washington ; 5. In the compiled Biography of the Signers in the Pennsylvania Historical Society library, three 4° volumes valued at $2000.

ii. ENGRAVING, " by J. B. Longacre from a Portrait by G. Stuart." This is the illustration in Sanderson's *Lives*, First and Second Editions. It is slightly less than one-half the size of the previous.

iii. ENGRAVING, " by T. B. Welch, from a painting by G. Stuart." " M. Quig printer." This illustrates the *National Portraits* by Longacre and Herring ; vol. for 1839 ; and also the second edition, by Rice and Hart 1854.

iv. ENGRAVING, " by S. C. Atkinson," [Apparently a copy

of Stuart] which illustrates Conrad's edition of Sanderson's *Lives*, 1 vol. imp 8° 1846 ; and also Benner's Dutch edition, 1842–58.

v. PRINT by Tiebout, in possession of the Pennsylvania Historical Society, entitled "Thomas McKean Governor of Pennsylvania, Published by D. Kennedy 228 Market St." The likeness shows the right side of the face; and is not familiar, to those who know Stuart's and the engravings from it. In its general appearance it resembles Peale's (No. 4), but in the details it does not; the expression is different from Peale's Portrait.

vi. ETCHING of the last named, by Albert Rosenthal, Philadelphia, forming the illustration to "*Philadelphia and the Federal Constitution.*"

vii. August 1781 "A profile in black lead of the pres. of Congress Thos. McKean, form of a medal," Extract from the note book of P. E. Du Simitiere in *Penn. Mag.* xiii. 367. The whereabouts of this likeness is not now known.

viii. CENTENNIAL MEMORIAL OF AMERICAN INDEPENDENCE ; by the American Bank Note Company, (30¼ in. by 19¾ in.) This large engraving contains the Declaration, several historical scenes connected with it, etc., Thomas McKean after Stuart, being one of the few likenesses here shown.

ix. THE FRONTISPIECE of the present work is a reproduction of David Edwin's engraving (No. i.) by the Moss Engraving Company of New York, and reduced one-half size. The autograph is from Stone's *fac-simile* of the Declaration, mentioned, *ante* pp. 48, 49.

Wood cuts illustrating various works, some of them very good likenesses, and generally after Stuart, are numerous ; but no list of them has been made.

GOVERNOR McKEAN'S AUTOGRAPH AND LETTERS.

Thomas McKean's autograph is not a rare one compared with others of the Signers: Autograph hunters have succeeded in collecting twenty-two complete sets of autographs of the Signers; and it is not likely that any other complete set will ever be made, owing to the scarcity of one or two of the signatures.[1] Notices of some of these collections with fac-similes, including a sample of Governor McKean's writing, may be found in *Harper's Magazine* vol. xlvii. 258, 424, *et*

---

[1] Lyman C. Draper, in *Col. State Hist. Soc. of Wis.*, vol. x.

seq. The most valuable and interesting letter of Thomas McKean may be found in *fac simile* in the *Book of the Signers*, by William Brotherhead, Phila. 1861. The original, now or lately in possession of T. M. Rodney Esq., is dated Philadelhipa, August 22, 1813, and refers to his name being omitted in the first published copies of the Declaration, his sending an express for Cæsar Rodney, and his writing the Constitution for the State of Delaware in one night, without the aid of books or papers.[1]

Comparatively few letters of Thomas McKean have been quoted in this biography; Sanderson's *Lives* contains other letters and extracts not here quoted. A number of letters to and from Thomas McKean may be found in the *Works of John Adams* by his grandson Charles Francis Adams, 10 vols. 1856. Eight letters published by John Adams may be found in *Niles' Register*, vol. xii, p. 305, *et seq.* In the *Correspondence of the Revolution*, 4 vols. Boston 1853, and in the *Diplomatic Correspondence of the Revolution*, 4 vols. Boston 1829, both by Jared Sparks, are several letters, some of them addressed to Washington. A valuable letter to William McCorkle, June 16, 1817, may be found in *Niles' Register* vol. xii, 278, and also in the *Extracts from the Diary of Christopher Marshall*, William Duane, Albany 1877; in reference to the omission of his name on the copies of the Declaration. Several letters may likewise be found in Hazard's *Pennsylvania Colonial Records*, 16 vols. and its continuation, the *Pennsylvania Archives*, 12 vols. by Linn and Egle, published by the state, 1852–3. Other letters are scattered among various biographies, and other works.

In the Department of State at Washington are at least ninety-eight letters of Governor McKean, but few of which have probably been published. Eighty-eight of these were written while President of Congress, and are addressed among others to Samuel Huntington, Gens. Greene, Washington, Lafayette, Stark, Heath, Lincoln, Marion, Schuyler; Govs. Hancock, Clinton, Trumbull, Nelson, Burke; Presidents Reed, Rodney, the President of New Hampshire; also to M. de Marbois, Dr. Franklin, William Bingham, The People of New Hampshire, Hon. R. R. Livingston, The Minister of France,

---

[1] This letter was read by the Hon. Thomas F. Bayard, in his address on the occasion of the unveiling of the monument to Cæsar Rodney, at Dover, Del., October 30, 1889. The author kindly sent me a printed copy of the *Proceedings* containing his address; but it was received too late to be inserted in the note on page 29.

Thomas Jefferson, Count Rochambeau, Michael Hillegas, Count de Grasse. Also six other letters to General Washington, one of which, dated Newark October 8, 1777, is quoted in these pages from *Sparks' Correspondence of the Revolution.* These letters are not generally accessible unless copies are requested. .

BIBLIOGRAPHY.

A list of all works I have met with, which contain a biography of Thomas McKean, is appended to this genealogy, (Appendix I). Many of them are however copies of one another. In the appendix may also be found a list of official publications closely connected with the life of Thomas McKean. Other works containing merely mention of him are too numerous to be named, but references to them may be found in the notes to the foregoing biography.

Of these biographies, a few only need special mention as being well written, or containing facts not given in the other works, namely:

1. Sanderson's *Lives* 1820–7, and subsequent editions; 2. Judson's *Biography of the Signers*, 1839, a beautifully written article; 3. *National Portraits*, an article signed T. A. B. (author unknown), well written, but containing numerous mistakes in dates. 4. Nevin's *Continental Sketches of Distinguished Pennsylvanians*, 1875. 5. Armor's *Lives of the Governors of Pennsylvania*, 1872. 6. Hazard's *Register*, iii. 241—The Supreme Court Bench of Pennsylvania; 7. Scharf and Westcott's *History of Philadelphia* 3 vols. 4°, 1884, containing also very numerous references, and facts not elsewhere published.

CONCLUSION, GOVERNOR McKEAN'S CHILDREN.

Governor McKean's second wife survived him but three years, and died on Saturday, May 6, 1820, aged seventy-three years; and was buried on the 7th in the grave yard of the First Presbyterian Church. An oil portrait of her by Stuart is in possession of His Excellency the Marquis de Casa Yrujo, Madrid, Spain; and another by Charles Wilson Peale, noted on a previous page, is the property of Henry Pratt McKean, Esq., of Philadelphia.

All of Governor McKean's children are named in his bible record, owned by Mr. Henry Pratt McKean; and also the first

six in another record in possession of Miss Anna M. Bayard.
They are as follows:
By his first wife Mary Borden:

i.   JOSEPH BORDEN, b. Sunday, July 28, 1764.
ii. ROBERT,   b. Sunday, March 9, 1766.
iii. ELIZABETH,   b. Tuesday, August 18, 1767 (Mrs. Andrew
                       Pettit).
iv. LETITIA,   b. Friday, January 6, 1769 (Mrs. George Buch-
                       anan).
v.   MARY,   b. Monday, February 18, 1771; d. Thursday, De-
                       cember 27, 1781 ; buried in burial ground
                       of First Presbyterian church.
vi. ANNE,   b. Thursday, February 25, 1773 (Mrs. Andrew
                       Buchanan).

By his second wife, Sarah Armitage :

vii. A Son,   b. Wednesday, November 1, 1775 ; d. the same
                           day.
viii. SARAH,   b. Monday, July 8, 1777 ; baptized by Rev. Jo-
                           seph Montgomery (The Marchioness de
                           Casa Yrujo).
ix.   THOMAS,   b. Saturday, November 20, 1779, Philadelphia;
                           bapt. Jan. 30, 1780.[1]
x.   SOPHIA DOROTHEA, b. Monday, April 14, 1783, Philadelphia ; bapt.
                           July 27, 1783 ;[1] d. December 27, 1819 ;
                           bur. First Presbyterian church.
xi.   MARIA LOUISA,   b. Wednesday, September 28, 1785, Philadel-
                           phia ; bapt. Jan. 30, 1786 ;[1] d. Tuesday,
                           October 21, 1788 ; bur. First Presbyterian
                           church.

[1] These baptisms are from register of First Presbyterian church, Phila.

APPENDIX I.

LIST OF BOOKS CONTAINING BIOGRAPHIES OF THOMAS McKEAN, AND OTHER WORKS.

[WORKS CONTAINING MERE MENTION OF THOMAS McKEAN, COMPRISING THE GREATER PART OF THOSE REFERRED TO IN THE FOOT NOTES, AND NUMBERING ABOUT 200, ARE NOT INCLUDED IN THIS LIST.]

Sanderson's Biographies of the Signers.

Biography of the Signers of the Declaration of Independence, John Sanderson, 9 vols. Phila. R, W. Pomeroy, 1820–7. Engraving by J. B. Longacre. Robert Waln is the biographer of Thomas McKean and of many other of the signers. This is the earliest work and the original of all the subsequent Lives of the Signers; and is still the standard work of its kind. Being published at first anonymously, it has been sometimes called "*Pomeroy's Lives.*"

(Rather singularly I have found a great variety in the title pages. One set dated 1820–7; a second 1823–7; a third 1823–4; Sanderson's name is given in some volumes, and not in others of the same set. On an engraved title page some volumes have a coiled serpent, others a female figure.)

The same, 2d Edition, 5 vols. Philadelphia. Pub. by W. Brown and C. Peters, 1828. Engraving by J. B. Longacre. (A few minor changes made in this edition).

The same. 5 vols. Published by Bennet and Walton, 1831. (Word for word the same as the 2nd edition.) [Not illustrated.]

The same. Revised by Robert T. Conrad. 1 vol. Imp. 8°. Thomas Cowperthwait & Co. Phila. 1846. Engraving by S. C. Atkinson.

The same as the last named. With 60 engravings, collected and prepared by William Brotherhead, 1865. 1 vol. 4°. 160 copies. $20.00. [Illustrated with a picture of Duché's house, but no engraving of Thomas McKean.] ·

Edition of Sanderson by Fowle, 1864. 607 pp., rough edges, $81. [Mentioned by Allibone.]

Lives of the Signers, By other authors.

C. A. Goodrich, Lives of the Signers. New York, 1829. 1 vol., 12°. [Partly illustrated, no engravings of Thomas McKean.]
N. Dwight, Sketches of the Lives of the Signers, New York, 1830; 1 vol., 12°. [Not illustrated.]
L. Carroll Judson, Biographies of the Signers (Author a member of the Philadelphia bar). Phila., 1839. 1 vol., 8°. [Not illustrated. A beautifully written biography.]
B. J. Lossing, Lives of the Signers, 1848 and Phila., 1870, 1 vol. [Poor woodcut likeness.]
E. Benner, Lebensbeschriebungen sämmtlicher unterzeichner der unabhängigkeitz-Erklarung. (In Dutch, chiefly from Goodrich's Lives. Engraving by S. C. Atkinson from Stuart. 12°. Sumneytown, Penn. 1842 and 1858.
Book of the Signers. William Brotherhead, large folio, Phila., 1861, containing facsimiles of letters, etc. Duché's house is shown.
Centennial Book of the Signers. William Brotherhead, Phila., copyright 1872, folio. A similar work to the previous. A poor woodcut after Tiebout.
Biography of the Signers, 3 vols., large 4°, in the library of the Pennsylvania Historical Society, for which the Society paid $2000. This work is a compilation. Each leaf from Sanderson's Lives is set in a border of stout paper, and the work illustrated with engravings, views, autograph letters, etc., from various sources. Engraving, large size by David Edwin.
Lives of the Pres. U. S. with biog. notices of Signers of the Dec. of Ind.: Robert W. Lincoln, Brattleborough, Vt., 1839.

Other Biographies of Thomas McKean.

National Portraits, J. B. Longacre and James Herring, 4 vols., 4° (vol. iv., for 1839). Engraving by T. B. Welch. A good biography.
The same. D. Rice and A. N. Hart. 4 vols., 1854; (vol. iv.) Engraving by T. B. Welch.
Hazard's Register of Pennsylvania, vol. vi. (for 1830), 161, 177, 191, Sanderson's biography in full; also vol. iii. (1829), 241; the Supreme Court Bench of Pennsylvania.
Lives of the Governors of Pennsylvania, William C. Armor. Phila., 1872. Wood cut and autograph.
Scharf and Westcott, History of Philadelphia. 3 vols., 4°. Phila., 1884. Biography ii.. 1515, *et seq.*, and very numerous references throughout the whole work. Wood cut, good likeness.
History of Chester county, Penn., Judge John Smith Futhey and Gilbert Cope. 4°. Phila., 1881. Biography and wood cut, 644 *et seq.*

Illust. History of Penn., William II. Egle, 1870. Short sketch and likeness.

Pennsylvania and the Federal Constitution, John Bach McMaster and Frederick D. Stone. Phila., 1888. 8°. Short sketch and etching from an old print by Tiebout.

Scharf's History of Delaware, 2 vols. Phila., 1888, i. 567.

Sages and Heroes of the American Revolution, L. Carroll Judson, 2 vols., 1851.

Harper's Magazine, iii. 145, vii., 429, et seq., a short sketch and likeness; xlvii., 429 et seq., fac-simile of handwriting of various signers; lii. 871, anecdotes and a good wood-cut likeness.

Historical Mag. of Notes and Q. iv., 2d Ser., Nov. 1868, p. 209, short sketches of the signers and others, with copies of letters from an autograph collection.

History of Independence Hall, D. W. Belisle, Phila., 1859. short sketch.

Continental Sketches of Distinguished Pennsylvanians, David R. B. Nevin. Phila., 1875. 8°. A good biography.

Lives of Eminent Philadelphians, Henry Simpson, Phila., 1859.

Field Book of the Revolution, Benson J. Lossing, New York, 1852 (and various editions). 2 vols. Various references and short biography, ii., 871; likenesses of the signers, etc.

Pennsylvania Magazine, xi., 249, et seq. "The Federal Constitution," by William H. Egle. Sketches of members of the Convention. A good biography.

Life and Corresp. of George Read. William T. Read, Phila., 1870. A full biography of Thomas McKean, p. 332, et seq.

Notæ Cestrienses. From the Village Record, West Chester, Pa., 1860. No. 12 of a series of historical articles. A short biography.

Bordentown and its Environs. In the Bordentown Register, 1876. Historical articles by E. M. Woodward, chap. xii. The Borden Family, and a sketch of Thomas McKean.

Catalogue of Independence Hall, 1878. (For the use of visitors.) List of portraits and brief sketches of the Signers.

Baltimore American and Commercial Advertiser, date unknown, probably quoted from Sanderson, about 1827.

Biographical Dictionaries, etc.

Appleton's New Cyclopædia of Biography, 6 vols., 1887, a good sketch and likeness.

Biographical Encyclopædia of Pennsylvania, 1874.

New American Cyclopædia, 16 vols. New York, 1875.

Allibone's Dictionary of Authors. 3 vols. A brief sketch.

Dictionary of Congress, Charles Lanman. (Published by Congress.) 5th Ed., 1868.

Biographical Annals of the U. S. Government, Charles Lanman, 2d Ed., 1887.
Drake's Dictionary of American Biography, Boston, 1872.
Allen's American Biographical Dictionary.
Political Register and Congressional Directory, B. P. Poore, Boston, 1878.
Appleton's Cyclop. of Biog., 1 vol., 1868, p. 558, brief sketch, improperly indexed.
Harper's Popular Cyclop. of U. S. History, N. Y., 1881, 2 vols.
Johnson's New Illust. Cyclop., N. Y., 1878, 4 vols. 4°.

Official Publications.

Journals of Congress, 13 vols. Pub. by authority, Phila., 1777, and subsequent ed.
Secret Journals of Congress, 4 vols. Pub. by Congress, 1821.
Debates on the Federal Constitution, Jonathan Elliot, 4 vols., published with the sanction of Congress, Washington, 1854.
Reports of Cases in Pennsylvania, A. J. Dallas, 4 vols., 1790–1807. Dedicated to Chief Justice McKean.
Pennsylvania Colonial Records, 16 vols. Pub. by the State, 1852–3.
·Pennsylvania Archives, 12 vols., Hazard, 1853.

Works by Governor McKean.

Laws of Newcastle, Kent and Sussex on Delaware, 1753–62, By authority of the General Assembly, by Thomas McKean and Cæsar Rodney. And laws down to 1777. Wilmington, 1763–77. Catalogued at the library of the Supreme Court of the United States, with a note, "believed to be the first book printed in Delaware." See page 14 *ante.*
Acts of the General Assembly of the Commonwealth of Pennsylvania, etc., by Thomas McKean, 1782, known briefly as *McKean's Laws.* See page 73 *ante.*
Charge of Thomas McKean, Chief Justice, to Grand Jury at Court of Oyer and Terminer, and General Gaol Delivery, held at York in 1788. (Hildeburn's Issues Phil. Press 1886, No. 3738.) See page 61 *ante.*
Commentary on the Constitution of the United States by Thomas McKean and James Wilson, London, 1792. See page 81 *ante.*
Speech [to the Legislature, Dec. 8, 1808], no title page, 8°. (Boston Ath. Cat.)

APPENDIX II.

MISTAKES AND DISCREPANCIES IN PRINTED BOOKS REGARDING GOVERNOR THOMAS McKEAN.

Sanderson's Lives. Adm. bar Chester co., 1755, not 1756; and Sup. Ct., 1758, not 1757.—Meeting at Carpenter's Hall in 1776, Franklin was not on the committee with Mr. McKean.—Vote on Res. of Independence taken July 2d, not 1st.—Mr. McKean signed Dec. Ind. in Jan. 1779, or later, not Oct. 1776.—Mr. Mc-Kean was not president of Delaware when appointed Ch. Justice, the office devolved upon him afterwards.—Const. of Delaware written at *Newcastle*, not *Dover.*—Mr. McKean moved to ratify Const. of U. S. on 24th, not 26th (See *Elliot's Debates*).—Mr. McKean m. 1st, July 21, 1763, not July, 1762.—wife died March 12, 1773, not Feb. 1773.—He m. 2d, Sept. 3, 1774, which was *Saturday*, not *Thursday.*—Age at death, 83 y., 2 m., 25 days, not 16 days.

Goodrich's Lives. Continental Cong. met Sept. 5th, not 3rd, 1775.

Journals of Congress and *Articles of Confederation*, discrepancy in date of ratification mentioned in the text (p. 65).

Declaration of Independence. Arguments to show that John Hancock and Charles Thomson did not sign it on July 4th, 1776, as generally stated by historians (p. 31, *et seq.*)

National Portraits, 1839. Mr. McKean served in Del. Assembly till 1779, not 1777.—Stamp Act Cong. met 1765, not 1768.—Com. to prepare Art. Confed., 1776, not 1775.—Loan Comms. till 1776, not 1772.—Justice of Peace, 1765, not 1768.—Art. Confed. agreed to 1777, not 1776.—Also Sanderson's mistakes in dates of m., d. and age are here copied.

Etting's *Old State House*, Lossing's *Field Book of Rev.*, Scharf and Westcott's *Hist. Phila.*, and Schart's *Hist. Md.*, give but *twelve* names on committee to prepare Art. Confed.; there were *thirteen*, one from each State (see text, p. 65).

Armor's *Lives of Govs. of Pa.*, and Scharf and Westcott's *Phila.* Mr. McKean b. *New London*, not *Londonderry.*

(129)

Scharf and Westcott's *Phila.*, p. 446. Conv. to ratify Const. of U. S. met Nov. 20th, not 21st.

Elliot's *Debates on Fed. Const.*, ii, 417. Mr. McKean moved to ratify Const. U. S. on Saturday, 24th, not 26th ; Bancroft points out this mistake.

Appleton's *Cycl. of Biog.* McKean and Wilson's Commentary on Const. U. S., published 1792, not 1790.

Bancroft's *Hist. U. S.*, 1876, v. 355, and 1885, v. 16, states that Mr. McKean signed the Declaration in 1781. I think it undoubtedly a mistake, although Mr. Bancroft in reply to my inquiries kindly informs me that he believes it to be correct—that it is not a misprint. This date is copied in Winsor's *History* and in Judge Chamberlain's *Authentication.*

Life of George Read. William T. Read, 1870, several mistakes in dates, etc. (p. 53 note.)—Claim that George Read wrote Const. of Del. not substantiated (p. 52–4).

Watson's Annals (Hazard's Ed.), and *Potter's Am. Monthly*, mistakes as to Dec. Ind. corrected (p. 33, note).

Poetical Addresses. G. A. Townsend, Cæsar Rodney's 4th of July. For *John* McKean read *Thomas* McKean; the latter name, it will be noticed, does not suit the. metre of the poem. The author kindly informs me that the character· *Sarah Rowland* in the poem is a fiction—an invention for detaining Mr. Rodney.

Histor. Mag. iv, 2d Ser., 209, *et seq.* A sketch of Mr. McKean contains several inaccuracies.

Lincoln's *Lives Pres. U. S. and Signers*, states wrongly that Mr. McKean was present in Congress, Aug. 2d, and signed Dec. Ind. on that day.

Hildrith's *Hist. U. S.*, v. 328, vote for governor in 1799, the votes for McKean and for Ross are each 10,000 too small.

The vote for governor at McKean's first election is thus stated by Mr. Herman P. Miller, in the office of the Pa. Senate, in a letter of Dec. 4, 1889. A mistake of 792 in the return of Chester co. made McKean's vote 37,244; corrected the next day in the Senate to be 38,036. Ross's vote was 32,643, not 32,641, as in Cochran's *Handbook.*

Cochran's *Handbook of Pa.*, 1889, gives the three votes thus:—

1799.		1802.	
Thomas McKean, Dem.,	38,036	Thomas McKean, Dem.,	47,879
James Ross, Federal,	32,643	James Ross of Pittsburgh,Fed.,	9,499
[The mistake in Ross's vote is		James Ross, Federal,	7,538
here corrected.]		Scattering,	94

1805.	
Thomas McKean, Independent Democrat,	43,644
Simon Snyder, Democrat,	38,483
Simon Snyder,	395

Burlington and Mercer Co., and in *Bordentown Register*, 1876, E. M. Woodward. The progenitor of Borden family is *Richard*, not *Benjamin.*—Joseph Borden m. Elizabeth Rogers, not a dau. of Marmaduke Watson.—Mr. McKean d. June 24th, not 4th. *Genealogy of the Roberdeau Family*, p. 137. Borden pedigree, the date of 1763–5 belongs to the previous generation.—Mary Borden m. 1763, not 1762. Lætitia McKean b. 1769, not 1770; m. June 11th, not 10th.—Gen. A. Buchanan b. 1734, not 1732, and d. 1786, not 1785.

ADDENDA ET CORRIGENDA.

16, l. 2, I find that Savage gives the date of baptism; his date of birth may therefore be more reliable than that deduced from the Borden record.

16, l. 3, 1614 should be 1610.

18–19, From the Address of the Hon. Thomas F. Bayard, published in the *Proceedings on Unveiling the Monumemt to Cæsar Rodney*, at Dover, Oct. 30, 1889, p. 24, I find that the incident here related is from a letter of Thomas McKean to John Adams, Aug. 20, 1815.

19, note 3, for Adam's read Adams'.

22, l. 25, *et seq.*, Compare a letter of Cæsar Rodney to his brother Thomas, Aug. 28, 1776, Force's *Am. Archives*, V. i. 1192.

28, note 4, for *Scharf and Westcott*, p. 321, read p. 312.

39, Plate and in Preface. The clauses in the Domestic Journal which are omitted in the published copies, may be found in Force's *American Archives*, IV. vi, 1731; in which is given what is more properly the *Proceedings* in Congress than a *Journal*, for it is compiled from various sources. When writing pages 41 *et seq.* of the text, I did not know the high authority attaching to these clauses; or I should have made use of another argument which they furnish, to prove that John Hancock had nothing to do with the preparation or authentication of the printed broadside. The resolutions are not addressed to him either personally or as President of Congress, and moreover it will be remarked that the expression here made use of is not that the declaration be *signed* but *authenticated*.

46. The letter of Cæsar Rodney above referred to, *Am. Archives*, V. i, 1192, gives the exact dates when Thomas McKean returned to Philadelphia from the army, and when he left for

Newcastle. The letter is dated Phila., Aug. 28, 1776, and states that Mr. McKean arrived on *Sunday night last*, and left yesterday morning. This date, I have computed, fell upon *Wednesday;* he therefore arrived on the 25th and left on Tuesday the 27th.

48–9. Stone's fac-simile of the Declaration. In the *Annals of Congress,* Gales and Seaton, (18 Cong. 1st ses. 1823–4, vol. i. 82, 431, 779, 915 ; ii. 2711) it is stated that under date of Jan. 1, 1824, John Quincy Adams, then Secretary of State, informs the Senate and House that an exact fac-simile of the Declaration has been made on copper, and 200 copies struck off, which are at the disposal of Congress. By resolution, these were distributed— two copies each to the surviving Signers, to the Marquis de Lafayette, to the President, to the late President Mr. Madison, etc., etc. But three signers were alive at this time ; and Sanderson in his life of Charles Carroll mentions the copy sent to that gentleman. The copy in possession of Commodore McKean's family, can now be identified as one of these, and I am informed that there is a tradition in the family that it is one of a number distributed to the Signers. Inquiry at the State Department elicits the fact that the copper plate is not now in the possession of the Department and its whereabouts is unknown.

65, note 1, Add to the list of works containing but *twelve* names, Scharf's *Hist. Maryland,* 1879, ii. 465.

81, note 2, for vol. iii, read ii.

82, l. 2, for Ingersol, read Ingersoll.

117, l. 11, for two, read too.

INDEX OF PRINCIPAL SUBJECTS.

www.ingramcontent.com/pod-product-compliance
Lightning Source LLC
Chambersburg PA
CBHW021134020726
47500CB00003B/1080